"No Point Hiding Your Reaction To Me, Lily."

Her eyes narrowed in contradiction, but her chest moved in rapid, shallow breaths.

A smile of victory threatened, but he let only one corner of his mouth curve up. "Don't worry, there will be time for that. A lifetime of opportunities."

Gasping, Lily stepped back, rubbing her palms over the skin he had held. "No, Damon. I agreed to marry you. I agreed to have your baby, which it so happens I'm already carrying. But I did *not* agree to share your bed. It won't be that type of marriage."

The smile playing on his lips extended into a full-blown version. A challenge. He loved a challenge if the prize was worth winning. And this woman in front of him was worth bedding— he knew that well.

Dear Reader,

I love a reunion story—especially with a couple where the passion still runs deep. So it was such a pleasure to sink into Lily Grayson's life when she meets with her ex-lover, the rich and gorgeous Damon Blakely.

Having been brought up around art and galleries, it was natural for me to infuse Lily's life with touches of the art world through her job as a gallery curator. Monet's series of water lilies have always spoken to me, and Lily shares my appreciation (though Damon prefers a different series by Monet—one that more reflects his personality!).

As an avid reader of Silhouette Desire books, I'm thrilled my own first Desire novel is finally here. Lily and Damon's story will always hold that special "firstborn" place in my heart and I hope you enjoy reading it.

Best wishes,

Rachel

RACHEL BAILEY

CLAIMING HIS BOUGHT BRIDE

Silhouette Desire

Published by Silhouette Books

America's Publisher of Contemporary Romance

SILHOUETTE BOOKS

ISBN-13: 978-0-373-73005-6

CLAIMING HIS BOUGHT BRIDE

Copyright © 2010 by Rachel Robinson

Recycling programs
for this product may
not exist in your area.

Visit Silhouette Books at www.eHarlequin.com

Printed in U.S.A.

RACHEL BAILEY

developed a serious book addiction at a young age (via Peter Rabbit and Jemima Puddleduck) and has never recovered. Just how she likes it. She went on to gain degrees in psychology and social work, but is now living her dream—writing romance for a living.

She lives on a piece of paradise on Australia's Sunshine Coast with her hero and four dogs, and loves to sit with a dog or two, overlooking the trees and reading books from her ever-growing to-be-read pile.

Rachel would love to hear from you and can be contacted through her Web site, www.rachelbailey.com.

To my own personal hero, John.
For everything.

Thanks to

Diana Ventimiglia for believing in this book
and for her continued guidance.

Jennifer Schober for her faith in me.

Robyn Grady, Barbara Jeffcott Geris, Melissa James
and Sharon Archer for their brilliant critiquing.

One

Lily Grayson placed a hand on her still-slender waist and searched the familiar ballroom. Shimmering silver and gold streamers hung from the expansive twenty-foot ceiling; a string quartet provided presupper music, which blended with the chatter of two hundred black-tie guests. A high-society birthday party was in full swing, but enjoying the festivities could play no part in Lily's plan.

Lips dry and her breathing shallow, her gaze flew from face to face, looking for the man she needed to speak with urgently. The man she'd once loved, but could never trust with her heart…or their unborn baby's emotional well-being.

Damon Blakely.

The multimillionaire corporate raider whom men feared and women coveted.

A waiter paused, tray covered with flutes of crystalline champagne and fine-stemmed glasses of wine, but she shook her head and continued her circuit of Travis Blakely's sixtieth birthday party. In the six months she'd been with Damon, she'd visited his uncle's Melbourne home several times, but not once since their breakup almost three months ago. Since Damon had let her down when she'd needed him most.

The thought led back to her gran, home alone tonight, recovering from another bout of pneumonia, part of the ill health that had incapacitated her recently. If only Gran would accept more help, but she refused to move in with Lily or let Lily live with her. Gran valued her independence and Lily couldn't help but feel powerless. But she wouldn't be sidetracked with thoughts of her beloved grandmother now. She'd see Gran taken care of, one way or another.

Tonight she needed to find Damon.

Lily continued searching from guest to guest as she wove through the crowd. The women in evening gowns of satins and sequins reminded her of peacocks parading for attention, and the sounds of clinking glasses and a hundred indistinct conversations culminated in an assault on her ears. She'd rather be anywhere than here—this was not her world. But it was *his* world and she needed to find him.

Searching still, she swung around. Her heartbeat stalled before exploding in her chest as her gaze collided with his.

Dead ahead, suave in a tux, red wine in one hand, the other free to shake the hands of acquaintances who stepped into his path, Damon smiled and passed comments with those who waylaid him. The charming lord of all he surveyed. But his distinctive eyes, with the black ring circling the ice-blue iris, were focused on her.

An exquisite shiver passed down her spine at the intensity of his gaze and her body reacted with predictable awareness. Lily closed her eyes to tamp down the response but her lids immediately fluttered open. He stirred within her an overwhelming hunger. Even now, she couldn't keep her eyes from devouring him.

Damon towered over the other guests, and she realized that instead of searching for him, she should have stood on the entrance stairs to spot his characteristic waves of midnight-dark hair. Or closed her eyes and let her body find his with the magnetic link that still drew her to him.

He finished talking to a rotund man, who laughed heartily at Damon's parting comment, then took several strides toward her before being tapped on the shoulder by an elderly statesman Lily recognized from the newspapers.

She eased out a breath—it seemed she wouldn't need to approach him. He was coming to her. As her blood heated and skin tightened at the thought, she took an involuntary step back. Amazing. Even after all his neglect and the utter anguish he'd caused, the force of her attraction was still overpowering.

Leaning against a cool pillar, she waited, taking in the scene of Melbourne's elite at play. At odds with those around her, she'd never wanted a life of extravagance. Growing up with Gran, who'd struggled to keep a roof over their heads after her son—Lily's father—had gambled the family home away, she'd wished only for security. Financial stability, no more.

The cloying scent of too many expensive perfumes and colognes mingling in the enclosed space made her head spin, and she looked longingly toward the exit. She needed to get this over with. The stress of trying to anticipate Damon's reaction to her news was pushing her to breaking point. She was still coming to grips with it herself.

Finished with the statesman, Damon took the last few strides to reach her, his broad shoulders and long legs showcased by the tuxedo.

He didn't say a word, just seemed to drink her in, his sensuous mouth parted slightly before he downed the rest of his wine and discarded the glass on the tray of a passing waiter. Then he clasped her elbow and slowly reached down to press a kiss to her cheek, a little too close to the corner of her mouth for propriety, but then Damon had never worried about convention when it clashed with his interests.

"Hello, Lily." He seemed to roll her name around his mouth before delivering it in his deep voice, something that had always sent her pulse erratic. "You look gorgeous."

His compliment hummed through her blood, even as she told herself not to listen. She'd learned long ago that people said what they wanted you to hear. A lesson she'd relearned recently thanks to the man still holding her arm.

She swallowed and found her voice. "Hello, Damon. You look good, too. You always did in a tuxedo," she conceded.

His mouth curved and pale blue eyes gleamed. "I'd rather hoped you preferred me out of my tuxedo."

An unbidden image of them entwined on his bed rose in her mind. The memory of his tanned, muscled body contrasted against crisp fine cotton sheets made her inwardly groan. When an ache deep and low in her stomach began to throb, Lily gritted her teeth and withdrew her elbow in a move others in the room wouldn't notice, but which sent a clear message to Damon—touching was a right he no longer possessed.

A raised eyebrow told her he'd taken her meaning and wasn't offended. He sank his hands into his front trouser pockets. Confident and sexy to the core.

She needed to tell him now, before his lethal sexuality scrambled her brain further. Needed to get him somewhere private so she could tell him about their baby as well as her plans to move on with her life.

He leaned close and whispered in her ear, his warm breath tickling sensuously. "There's something I'd like to talk to you about in private."

Lily froze. Had he guessed? No, he couldn't have— she wasn't showing yet and at fourteen weeks, her morning sickness had passed. There were no clues and no one else knew, she'd made certain of it. Her secret was safe, until she told Damon in her own words.

And now he wanted to speak to her in private—it seemed fate had cut her a break for once. She would grab the opportunity. "When?"

He gave a self-satisfied grin. "How does now suit?"

Her legs felt weak but she maintained the cool facade. "Where?"

For reply he took her hand and led her away. As firecrackers shot through her veins, Lily shook her head.

Obviously she needed to make clearer her position on the no-touching rule. However, for expediency's sake, this one last time she would allow the contact.

Though perhaps she shouldn't take his acts of entitlement and their effects on her so personally; all women seemed to succumb to Damon Blakely's innate sensuality when they were in his orbit. Far more important to her were other qualities—traits Damon seemed incapable of understanding or displaying. Emotional reliability. Prioritizing others' needs before his own. Worse, she knew that would never change.

He drew her down a quiet hallway toward the rear of the stark mansion where he'd grown up, until she recognized the heavy double sliding doors of Travis Blakely's private gallery.

Damon flicked on the lights and her art-gallery curator's eye was drawn to the priceless artwork hanging on the walls and enclosed in glass on podiums.

She drifted forward and ran a finger along the edge of one glass cabinet, not turning to him, even when he spoke.

"We haven't been alone in, how long?" A wall of heat moved behind her and for one crazy moment she let herself simply absorb his warmth in hope of soothing her chilled heart.

"Almost three months." She turned, bringing her within a foot of him. Her heart skipped a beat to find him so close.

"How have you been? Your gran?" He casually reached to toy with a strand of her long silver-blond hair, sending a frisson of heat across her skin.

"I've been fine," she whispered, wishing her voice had been stronger but unable to help his effect on her.

"Gran's been under the weather, but she's coming out of it now."

At least physically. Her medical bills had mounted up and, with no assets or income besides the old age pension, Lily was worried for the woman who'd raised her since the age of twelve. Gran had already lost so much, her son, her health, her house, her nest egg…

Damon released the lock of hair and grazed his knuckles down the side of her cheek in a touch as light as butterfly wings. "That must have been hard for you."

Lily nodded, torn between her body's reaction to Damon's touch and the thoughts his words evoked. She owed Gran everything, loved her beyond measure.

"I suppose she still won't let you help." His voice was quiet, beguiling.

On the verge of slipping under his sensual thrall, she caught herself. She had to wrest back power over her own body.

She stepped away and moved to the other side of the glass cage, putting the artwork between them as a token symbol of protection. Only then did she trust herself to reply. "She says that after raising me to stand on my own two feet, the last thing she wants is for me to be financially behind the eight ball because of her."

Damon didn't appear to feel thwarted by her physical retreat, more like she'd thrown down the gauntlet and he'd accepted. He prowled the trail she'd followed, yet bypassed her position and leaned against a nearby column, ankles crossed, hands resting on narrow hips. The pose of a predator biding his time. "Have you come up with any options?"

She took a breath, held it, then admitted, "Not yet. But I will." Finding a way to look after Gran was a priority.

He pushed off the column, rolling his shoulders as he hunted the shadows of the room, before turning and ending squarely in front of her.

His eyes seemed to consume her whole. "You seem sure about that." His arched eyebrow told her that he didn't share her confidence.

Truth be told, she had no idea *how* she'd make sure Gran was taken care of, but she wouldn't consider failure.

"Don't worry about me, Damon, I'll find a way." The heat radiating from him, the raw sexual hunger in his gaze, made it difficult to think, to say anything, but she needed to change the subject. "It seems I should be more worried about you. I heard Travis disinherited you after we broke up."

"Ah, yes. The millions of tainted dollars, this loving family home." He swept an arm around, eyes filled with derision. "Everything."

"Including the one thing you've always coveted." *Had wanted more than he'd wanted her.* His late father's company, BlakeCorp.

Looking down at her hands, she blinked away any remnants of emotion that thought still evoked. She was over it. Over him.

Movement drew her attention back to his face. He was closer again. The barely visible tension in his features dissolved, replaced by his usual arrogant self-assurance.

Hands clasped behind his back, Damon leaned in to whisper in her ear. "I have an offer for you. To help your gran."

Undiluted shock surged through her entire body. Her neck snapped back and she sought his eyes. It was the last thing she'd expected. "What offer?"

"I'll buy her a house. One with all modern safety features for someone her age, but where she still has her independence. I'll pay off all her outstanding medical expenses. And I'll employ a private nurse to help until she's back on her feet. Longer, if she'll allow it." He smiled, assured his offer was too good to refuse. "You know she'll accept. She knows I can afford it and she always had a soft spot for me."

"Why would you do that?"

He shrugged and took her hand, drawing her still closer, pressing his advantage. "Travis invited me here tonight to make me an offer. I want to extend the offer to include you. And your Gran."

Lily narrowed her eyes. "I thought you'd both sworn never to lay eyes on the other again." In fact, she'd been astonished when Travis's secretary had rung to follow up on Lily's RSVP tonight, and had revealed that Damon was expected. But she'd immediately seen her chance to speak with him—Damon had been out of the country and, unsure of when he'd jet off again, she'd grabbed the first opportunity to see him she could.

But she had to stay on guard. Game playing came as naturally to the Blakelys as making money. "Why would Travis come to you now and make an offer?"

"Been keeping up on the family goings-on, Lily?" His thumb ran up and down on the wrist he held. "Perhaps you still have my best interests at heart."

Lily blew out a dismissive breath and withdrew her hand. Her stomach churned. How much more of this game could she take? "Damon, for pity's sake, cut the theatrics and answer my question."

He smiled—the slow smile of a panther assured of catching its prey. Though, just who he thought his prey was this time—her or Travis—she wasn't certain.

"Travis received some tragic news from his doctor today." Damon didn't even try to pretend that any news that was tragic for Travis would adversely affect him. There had been no love lost between the two long before she'd met either of them.

She knew Travis had raised Damon with more than an iron rod—he'd also used emotional abuse and deliberate neglect as tools to rear his older brother's son. Damon had never wanted to talk much about it, but it'd been easy enough to put two and two together—and the answer had broken her heart. Perhaps she'd given Damon one chance too many when they'd been together, knowing how he'd never really escaped the torment of his childhood. But she couldn't go on giving him chances now. Things had changed.

One thing she knew, Damon would never forgive Travis. What surprised her was that they'd lasted so long without either one destroying the line of inheritance.

She tried to gauge Damon's feelings from his expression but failed. "If he's talking to you again, the news is obviously something that's made him confront his mortality."

Damon nodded. "Despite retaining the services of the best cardiovascular surgeon in the country, last month's operation to repair his heart was unsuccessful. Test results that came in today confirmed it. And he's apparently not a good candidate for a heart transplant—lack of donors, his age and the mistreatment he's given the rest of his body have seen to that. He pressed them for a prognosis. They've given him twelve months to live."

Despite Travis's mistreatment of Damon as a child, she couldn't help feeling a pang of sympathy.

And sympathy for Damon, faced with losing the only family he had left, albeit an estranged and loathed family member. Impulsively she reached out and laid her hand on his forearm, stroking the material covering his golden-brown skin.

"Damon, I'm sorry."

He made a dismissive sound and clamped down on her hand with his free one—not allowing her sympathy, but not permitting her to break the contact, either. "Actually, there's good news come from this. He's prepared to revise his will."

Lily blinked several times. "He'll give you your father's company back?" Was that why Damon was at this party tonight?

A glint appeared in his eye. "That was my price."

She hesitated, holding off congratulating him on achieving his longtime ambition until she'd heard the cost.

"It seems Travis has become sentimental. He wants to leave a legacy to his family." Damon's scornful smile clearly showed his opinion of his uncle's change of heart.

Lily frowned in confusion. "He's leaving you everything?"

"No, he's still determined I'll never touch a penny of his money. But he offered to leave his entire portfolio of assets and cash to my child. He said my child will be rich." Damon's smile didn't reach his eyes. "He failed to take into account that any child of mine would be rich without his *generous* offer." He moved away, restless, tension radiating from him in waves she could almost feel, but the emotion was tightly leashed.

Any child of his? He was seriously thinking about children? She'd hoped that, despite his incredibly busy life, he'd want to play some role in their baby's upbringing—though not a role that could allow him to repeat the cycle of the Blakely's cold, emotionally harsh parenting style. Perhaps something more like a big brother. She'd assumed he wouldn't want more than that—he'd told her more than once he didn't want children.

He stopped before a portrait of a Victorian woman surrounded by children dressed as small adults, gazing at the figures as if they held secret wisdom.

"Your child?" Instinctively her hand went to her belly as she watched his broad, tense back. And then another thought struck—had she missed a vital piece of Damon's history where he already had a child?

He turned in a cold, almost casual way and faced her again, this time with several feet distance between them. "*If* I conceive a child before he dies."

Lily nodded, with a streak of intense, perverse joy that Damon had no other children before the one she carried.

No. She gritted her teeth. She had to stop letting possessive thoughts like these sneak through her defenses. They were counterproductive to her goals. She needed to tell him her news, ask his cooperation and keep both her baby and heart protected in the process.

Stray possessive thoughts could play no part in her future relationship with him. She needed her wits about her. She was prepared to provide for this baby if Damon rejected fatherhood or denied paternity; she earned a good wage as assistant curator at the gallery. But she'd hoped with all her heart he'd want to make sure his child had every advantage. It seemed from his comments he would.

Rich was another story though. She didn't want Damon's fortune. The Blakely family was a stellar example of how excessive wealth corrupted morals.

Her hand found the silver heart pendant at her throat. "What did you tell him?"

He looked at her, down his long, proud nose. "I said no."

The vision of the two Blakely lions squaring off earlier in the night was strangely compelling. "So that's when he offered you your father's company?"

"He dangled BlakeCorp as a bribe and then threw in a touch of blackmail. Told me he'd leave all his worldly goods to his cousin's son, Mark, if I refused. And Mark would break it up and sell everything to the highest bidder—as long as that bidder wasn't me, as per my dear uncle's directions."

Lily had met Mark once at a family dinner. He had the Blakely ruthless, money-hungry gaze and it had chilled her from across the table. "So how will you produce this baby?"

Curiosity made her ask. She knew she should tell him now about her pregnancy, but first she desperately wanted to know what plan he'd devised.

"Ah, good question. And it's not just *any* baby. He wants a legitimate heir." Damon lifted a sardonic brow.

She drew in one long breath. "You'll marry?"

"Which is where you come in." Suddenly he was close again, so close she could feel the heat from his body, smell the rich red wine on his breath. "I want to marry *you*." He clasped both her hands and smiled in a good imitation of reasonableness.

Lily's head swam and her throat felt thick. His complete disinterest in having children in the past had allowed a hope he'd let her raise their baby on her own. But things had changed.

The room around her began a slow spin. If she told him now about her pregnancy, nothing would stop his pursuit of her. He'd made a decision that he wanted a child. Her child. For the sake of BlakeCorp, not because of love or commitment.

Damon always got what he wanted.

She bit down on the rising panic—everything had veered out of control within short minutes. Her simple plan of doing the right thing and telling him about the baby, asking him for financial support, and looking for a mutually agreeable role he could play in the child's life was now a complicated tangle.

"Lily?" He lifted her chin with a finger. "If you marry me, you and your gran would both be taken care of beyond your wildest dreams."

Still she couldn't speak. Couldn't think.

"I know it's a lot to take in, but this will work very well for us." He leaned in to feather a kiss along her jawline.

Damon was a man others regarded as beyond powerful, but she'd known from the start that his greatest power was his ability to enthrall. To mesmerize her with negligible effort. The knowledge, however, was little protection. She felt herself falling…. His lips brushed the sensitive skin of her throat, leaving a decadently moist trail.

"There were things left—" he paused and nipped her earlobe "—unfinished between us last time. I'm not fond of unfinished business, Lily."

She swallowed hard. "You mean I left you and you hate losing."

She felt his mouth curve into a smile against her skin. "We were good together before," he said between smooth kisses along her throat. "A marriage between us could work."

Would it? Her knees felt boneless from the ministrations he was paying her neck. It was obvious sexual compatibility would never be a problem. But now she couldn't play *make a decent go of it* or just *try* it. Breaking up over him letting her down that last day might seem an overreaction to some, but that had merely been the last straw for their relationship. She remembered the disillusionment when he dropped her home on her birthday, halfway through a romantic dinner, because work had called. Another time, he'd become so immersed in a stock market fluctuation, he'd totally forgotten to meet her. It was a day she'd really needed him—the tenth anniversary of her parents' deaths. Both times he'd promised to make it up to her, and she supposed he had, but she'd learned Damon wasn't a person she could rely on to be there when she needed him most. And her obligation now was first and foremost to the tiny life dependent on her.

Her own mother had put her husband's needs ahead of her child's. As a professional gambler, Lily's father had needed to travel, mostly in poverty, and Lily had been dragged from place to place, craving stability, routine, reliability. Until the age of twelve, when she'd moved in with her grandmother, she'd known none.

This baby's needs came before hers or Damon's.

She needed to find a way to make this new development work for her.

"If I were to agree," she croaked out through her dry throat. She swallowed, willing her voice to work. "I have some conditions of my own."

His eyes widened slightly but he nodded. "Tell me."

"I'd marry you if it meant Gran would be taken care of." Lily stepped back and wrapped her arms around herself. She'd walk over broken glass for that sweet woman.

"I sense a 'but' coming." His mouth curved.

"But bringing a baby into the equation is a different matter entirely." She took a deep breath and stepped farther away, outside his aura. "I'd want to bring this baby up on my own. One thing I learned from living with my parents and then Gran is it's not the number of people in the family that matters, it's the capacity to love, and prioritize each other. To be emotionally reliable for each other." Gran would be there for her now, too, and that was all she needed.

She braced herself to explain, to tell him the truth. As their baby's father, he deserved it, and she needed him to understand. "I'd never cut you off from your own child, but you have to know already that your version of commitment isn't what a child needs. Your priorities..." She trailed off, not sure how to word it without causing offence. Not sure how to tell him she didn't want the cycle of the Blakely men's frozen hearts thrust upon her innocent baby.

Uncertain, she clasped her hands together in front of her belly. "We would work out beforehand what role you'd want to play. Visitation rights that don't interfere too much with your work."

Damon thrust his hands into his trouser pockets. "Visitation rights?" The look in his eyes said he had no intention of being that far removed from his child, but she pressed on.

"I also want to be financially stable enough to know that my child will always have a home and things he or she needs. You'll make an account for the baby, in my name. I need to be secure." Her own wage was enough if push came to shove, but this was a way to ensure her baby would never go without.

He nodded, eyes calculating as she spoke. "Go on."

"And lastly, I want a contract ensuring these conditions are met." She raised her chin, hoping he didn't argue this point because it was an absolute bluff—she was in too far to walk away. Her baby's needs were paramount.

"You don't trust me, Lily?" A rare emotion passed across his face, but she wasn't sure it was hurt. Far more likely he was mocking her.

"I'll marry you and have the baby you need, Damon, but I'll raise it on my own with money from both of us.

Sign a contract to that effect or you'll have to find someone else."

He rocked back on his heels, a smile playing around his mouth. "You drive a hard bargain. Good for you." The smile that had threatened finally broke free and this time it reached his eyes. "These are precisely the qualities I want in the mother of my child."

He stepped forward but she moved sideways, evading him. She was shaking inside and, knowing the negotiations were at a critical point, needed all the distance from his masculine solidness she could manage. "You haven't answered. Will you sign a contract with my conditions?"

He reached for her, playing to her weakness, but she again evaded and crossed her arms under her breasts. "Damon?"

His gaze rested on hers, intense and unwavering. "My child will grow up where he should—in my house with his mother and father."

She felt the blood drain from her face. Once Damon made up his mind, he was unwavering…and she had so little bargaining room. Her mind raced so fast she began to feel light-headed. She needed to find a way to give herself some emotional space in this arrangement.

But there was only one option, and she sent up a quick prayer that he agreed, because she couldn't back out of this deal now. "I'll concede to living in your home, but only on the condition that we have separate bedrooms. On opposite sides of the house."

One side of his mouth quirked. "Are you sure that's what you really want, Lily?"

Her body screamed *no,* even as her mind continued to fine-tune her position. "This will be a paper marriage—we'll live separate lives under one roof. I won't share your bed, Damon. Now or ever."

He chuckled with genuine amusement. "Ah, sweetheart, you're forgetting the child we need to make." He cast her a look that in the past would have made her come to him. "I'm looking forward to that part immensely."

Lily finally allowed herself to return the smile. She knew he'd try to change the parameters, turn the situation to his benefit, but at least if she could get him to sign a contract, she had a leg to stand on.

If only she felt as confident about resisting the invitation to his bed.

"As it happens, that won't be a problem," she said, laying her hands over her waist. "I'm already pregnant with your baby."

Two

Damon called up all his famed reserves of self-control to avoid swaying on his feet.

She was pregnant?

His head swam as if he'd been sucker punched. He supposed he had been. In all the preplanning and strategizing, he'd not once factored in this possibility. It had just never occurred to him that she already nurtured his baby inside her body.

His gaze fixed on her stomach, searching for answers. He found none, just her flawless pale fingers stretched across the narrow expanse of her waist.

Heart beating slower than usual with shock, mind trying to make sense of the new information, he lifted his eyes to meet hers. She stood very still; a serene mask covered her features. How could she be so calm after delivering news this momentous?

Then it came—the crack in Lily's veneer. She pulled one side of her full bottom lip between her straight white teeth and bit delicately down. He'd lost count of the number of people he'd played in his line of work, the number of meetings where he'd wrested control from unwilling board members. The key was always to wait until that small sign of unease appeared—to be able to recognize it—then to act without mercy.

Yet he remained unmoving, emotions frozen.

She was carrying his child?

Then, as if time caught up with crashing reality, his body came back to life. Heart pumped hard, mind cleared, adrenaline flowed.

He had a child. That baby in her womb *belonged to him.* He'd never considered children in his future, not until his uncle's ultimatum, but now that the reality presented itself, he knew he'd *never* let that child go.

Lily's condition of separate bedrooms be damned. He hadn't been prepared to sign his name to that idea even before her announcement, but now there was no way in hell he'd let her create distance between them. The baby and the woman carrying it were his and would stay that way no matter what he needed to do to ensure it.

He glanced over at her. She was exquisite with her forest-green eyes, her alabaster skin, her silver-blond hair glimmering under the soft light. He desired her like no other. Even since first meeting her at a gallery fund-raiser, she'd gotten under his skin. And now she'd be forever tied to him.

Unwilling to show her any of his innermost reactions, he spoke with little inflection to his words. "You played that card close to your chest, sweetheart."

"Not—" she cleared her throat "—not really. I suspected…thought I knew…but only had it confirmed by a doctor today. It's why I came here tonight. To find you and tell you." Her hands remained across her belly, almost protectively.

"So you were pregnant when you left me." His voice was flat, almost accusing, even to his own ears.

She grimaced. "I didn't know I was."

He raised a brow. The outcome was the same. And he had another question while they were on the topic. "Tell me honestly, Lily, why did you leave?"

With shaking hands, she pushed a strand of hair behind an ear. "Is there any purpose in dredging this up now?"

Maybe not, but the question had bothered him— pride had kept him from pursuing an answer. But now she was here in the flesh, he needed an answer. "We're getting married. I think a short analysis on the breakdown of our past relationship has relevance."

She lifted her chin, but ruined the effect by biting down again on her full bottom lip. "Because I was too low a priority in your life."

That again! He'd prioritized her above almost everything, higher than a woman had ever been, and she still wanted more?

Needing to move, to use some of the adrenaline hurtling through his veins, he strolled with controlled movements to look into a glass cage enclosing an ancient clay urn. Several museums had offered exorbitant amounts of money to buy the artifact, and yet here it'd stayed. Trapped by Travis in this mausoleum, the way Damon himself had been for many years.

Nothing mattered more to him than reclaiming his heritage. He'd been made to feel like a poor, pathetic relation, when his father's business savvy was the only reason Travis wasn't still working as a junior assistant somewhere. It was time to restore rightful order to the world.

He swiveled to face Lily, the only woman who'd ever sparked dreams that didn't include BlakeCorp. The innate sensuality in the way she moved; her mouth, made for such sweetness and such sin; her heart, so untainted by the blackness that consumed his.

But everything had changed. And he needed to be very clear about his priorities. This woman was the key to BlakeCorp...and his baby.

"We'll marry as soon as I can arrange it." He stepped forward and grasped her upper arms, ignoring his body's insistent response to her. His blood had heated the moment he saw her in the ballroom, and now his groin screamed for attention.

He heard her breath catch at the touch but she tried to smother it, to deny his power over her, simply nodding her answer.

He let his voice drop to the seductive timbre she always responded to. "No point hiding your reaction to me, Lily."

Her eyes narrowed in contradiction but her chest moved in rapid, shallow breaths.

A smile of victory threatened, but he only let one

corner of his mouth curve up. "Don't worry, there will be time for that. A lifetime of opportunities."

Gasping, Lily stepped back, rubbing her palms over the skin he had held. "No, Damon. I agreed to marry you. I agreed to have your baby, which it so happens I'm already carrying. But I did *not* agree to share your bed. It won't be that type of marriage."

The smile playing on his lips extended into a full-blown version. A challenge. He loved a challenge if the prize was worth winning. And this woman in front of him was worth bedding—he knew that well.

He let out a slow, easy breath and sank his hands into his trouser pockets. "Let's just see how things unfold."

"I know how things will unfold. We'll be married in name only. We might live under the same roof, but we will be living separate lives. I let you hurt me before when I relied on you, needed you. And every time you had to choose between your business and me, you chose it, no matter how high my needs were or how minor the work issue. Be warned, I won't be as naive this time."

He waved her claim away. "Ancient history. We're starting anew. Something I'm very much looking forward to." He brushed a kiss on her cheek and held out his arm to escort her back to the party. After a brief hesitation, she raised her chin and preceded him out the doors.

He watched her go, appreciating the shape of her back, the sway of her hips.

Nothing would stop him from claiming his child or his father's company—they rightfully belonged to him. And he had a burning need to have this woman under him again. Fate had conveniently wrapped all the things he wanted in one neat, sweet-smelling package.

All he must do was coax his bride-to-be back into his bed.

The following morning, Lily wandered through the crowd of art-lovers as they milled around the display of Impressionist paintings her gallery was showcasing.

This exhibition had been her special project—selecting the paintings she wanted to show together, arranging with interstate and international galleries to borrow artwork to complement their own examples of the style, organizing events with schools and the public to coincide with the opening week. And she'd loved every minute.

She continued her stroll. The sounds of a busy exhibition always pleased her—the muffled footsteps on the tiled floor, voices raised or lowered in wonder and awe, an occasional guide sharing their passion.

Blended with that was the knowledge that today was the second to last day, giving her a twinge of sadness that usually came with the end of an exhibition. From tomorrow night, they'd begin taking down the display, returning paintings, completing paperwork. In a few days' time, another exhibition would fill this room.

Lily paused to appreciate some of her last moments with her favorite Monet. One of his series of water lilies, it was incredibly popular with the crowds for its lavenders, greens, pinks and blues—its undeniable intensity and luminosity.

But she loved this series because it showed the multitude of ways there were to look at the same subject, depending on time of day, the season or the position of the observer.

Similarly, there were many ways to view marriage: a fairy tale come true with hearts and flowers; a deep commitment with a soul mate that transcended the mere institution…or a pragmatic contract used to secure an inheritance.

She'd never yearned for the trappings of a fairy tale, but, despite her parents' train-wreck of an example, she'd always secretly hoped that somewhere she had a soul mate and they'd eventually find each other.

Marriage to Damon was not such a union.

As the reality of her situation hit her again, the room around her rocked then swooped, leaving her feeling faint.

Oh, God, what had she done?

"The water lily collection always struck me as overly sentimental," a deep voice said close to her ear.

She turned quickly to see Damon staring at the Monet, hands on hips, bunching the sides of his dark gray suit jacket above them.

"I like his series of the French cathedral more," he said, gaze still on the artwork. "Same concept of capturing the subject in different lights, but a much more interesting outcome."

She inhaled an intoxicating breath of his spicy scent. He always smelled so damn good. She'd noticed his cologne on other men and it'd had nowhere near the bone-melting impact it did when blended with Damon's own scent.

With effort, she brought her attention back to the conversation on art. "Buildings are more interesting than flowers and nature?" Though, she knew the answer from Damon's point of view. The material, the concrete, the financially tangible were always more valuable than simple beauty. What *did* interest her was his apparent knowledge of the French Impressionist. When they'd met, he'd claimed to have little understanding of the art world.

He turned, taking in her expression, and raised a brow—a look made all the more devilish by the accompanying heavy-lidded gaze. "I like buildings. And don't look so shocked that I recognize the painting. If you date someone with a PhD in fine art for six months, something's bound to rub off."

Lily laughed softly, conceding the point. "So now you're a gallery regular?"

"No, I've come to see my fiancée." He cupped her chin and brushed a kiss across her lips. "I always did prefer snow lilies to their watery cousins."

Words of praise dripped so easily from his tongue— with or without sincerity—that she refused to respond. She'd fallen for his silver-tongued flattery before. It had led to heartache whenever he left her without looking back. She must not forget.

And yet a part of her she couldn't control craved his kiss, craved *him* beyond reason.

He released her chin and dropped his hand into his trouser pocket. "And to finalize some arrangements. How soon can you get time off work?"

Her mind clicked into gear, pushing aside any remnants of hurt that he could so easily, so clinically, switch topics of discussion. It was only what she'd expected. Men like Damon did not while away the time talking about paintings. They mentioned them as a lead-in to getting what they wanted. Another reminder not to let down her guard.

Instead, she began thinking through the question and implications. This exhibition was almost over and she'd be going into detailed planning of her next project—a good time to take a day or two off if necessary to organize legal documentation for their wedding. "What do you have in mind?"

He rocked back on his heels, all casual confidence. "We fly out to New Zealand in three days, exchange vows and fly back. You'll need a week off work to cover the flights and a couple of days there."

Her stomach lurched. She seemed to have missed a step. "New Zealand?"

He lifted his shoulders then dropped them in a confident gesture. "Much quicker than waiting for the paperwork to go through in Australia. I originally considered Las Vegas, but decided the shorter flights to and from Auckland will be better for the baby."

A group of gallery patrons gathered about the Monet so, feet on autopilot, Lily moved away toward the middle of the room. Damon followed.

Her mind whirred too fast for any one thought to be clear. She needed time; he was moving so fast. It hadn't even been twenty-four hours since she'd agreed to marry him, and now here he was, asking her to leave the country in three days.

Her lungs labored to draw in enough oxygen. "Can I think about it?"

"Sure." One corner of his mouth lifted in an incomparable show of self-satisfaction. "I've already booked the flights so there's no rush to secure seats."

The world stilled as a strong sense of déjà vu settled over her. This was what it'd been like to be involved with Damon Blakely the last time. She sometimes wondered why she hadn't seen these warning signs when they'd first met. The cavalier attitude to other people's plans and choices. The belief he knew better, that his decisions weighed more than those of mere mortals. The same warning signs her mother should have noticed in her father.

Defensive anger rose to fill her chest. "You booked tickets without checking with me first?"

The best seats, too, she knew without asking. The man had gall for an expensive gamble like that. But then he wouldn't have seen it as a gamble—he always got what he wanted.

He lowered his voice and his eyes darkened, the pupils expanding to almost meet the black ring around his ice-blue irises. "This is a priority for both of us. We need to make sure our baby is legitimate."

The anger dissolved as quickly as it'd arrived, leaving her deflated, empty. He was right. They did need to ensure the baby was legitimate for the terms of the will. She'd cede on this one point, but only because it made sense, not because of his tactics.

"I'll need to check with the gallery director." She shook her head and began heading for the staff offices, Damon almost a step ahead even when she led. "I'll let you know by tonight."

He dropped a casual arm around her shoulders, which she knew would be more to stop her walking in another direction than a gesture of affection. "Come to my place after work and tell me what you've arranged. You haven't seen my new house yet." His voice had deepened into black velvet.

He'd changed tactics, turned on the charm. Her mind could acknowledge the game plan in this move but her body reacted to the timbre of his voice with primal hunger down low in her belly.

The gleam in his eye told her he knew exactly the effect he was causing. He pressed his advantage, fingers caressing the exposed skin of her upper arm where his hand hung. She kept walking, trying desperately to control her rampant hormones that urged her to turn to him, to let him charm and seduce her, no matter the cost.

But no, the stakes were too high now. His agenda wouldn't have their baby as first priority and that was the *only* agenda she could approve at the moment.

She stiffened and pointedly tipped her chin to his hand as it lazily stroked her sensitized skin.

Never slow on the uptake, Damon dropped his arm— but let it trace a lazy path down her back as he did so.

Damon always held himself in such control she wondered for the hundredth time if he'd shown any genuine feeling—besides desire—in all their time together.

Dismissing the thought, she waited for the next tactic he'd pull out of the bag. The wait was short.

"Melissa is cooking pasta tonight." His tone was casual, as if he were doing her a favor. "She'd love to see you again."

Lily thought of Damon's housekeeper with her bush

of light brown curls and ready smile. "I'd like to see her again, too, but I'm pretty tired these days after work."

She was past the morning sickness stage and now the main side effect of her pregnancy seemed to be fatigue. Besides, she needed as much distance from Damon as she could get. Distance seemed to be the only effective strategy in resisting him, and even then its value was questionable. "I'd rather ring and have an early night."

Immediately, his expression morphed into concern and he swung around in front of her, blocking her path. "Are you getting enough rest?" He clasped her elbow. "Perhaps this job is too much for you in your condition."

Resisting the urge to roll her eyes, she hooked the sides of her hair behind her ears and took a deep breath before answering. "Damon, I'm fine. I'm a little tired from the pregnancy, but nothing to be alarmed about. I'm more than capable of doing my job."

Though the thought *had* crossed her mind that if she was this tired at three and a half months, how would she cope at eight months? Or after the birth when she'd be struggling with disrupted sleep? She had no experience of babies, of motherhood, and that deficiency scared her.

He considered a moment then nodded with deceptive slowness. "Fair enough. I'll bring Melissa's pasta to you. What time will you get home?"

Her heart pinched tight. Despite his high-handed manner, it was nice to have someone other than her grandmother worry about her—even if it was only to guard an investment. So she smiled her gratitude even as she rejected his offer. "I'll be fine. I made a big pot of soup last night and there's some still in the fridge. I'll heat that."

She sidestepped him and continued toward the restricted access area.

Without missing a beat, he was beside her, matching her strides. "Soup? Does that have everything a baby needs?"

A gallery staff member walked past and waved. Damon watched Lily wave back but felt her tense beside him and instinctively knew her reaction was about his question not the colleague. He frowned. She didn't like him helping?

She kept walking. "I appreciate your concern, but I can look after myself." Her voice was calm and only a tinge of exasperation laced her words. "And now I have to go back to work." They'd arrived at the doors to staff offices. "So if you'll excuse me, I'll call you tonight."

He nodded, watched her swipe her security badge and walk through the door.

She was wrong. Someone needed to look after both her and his baby. And he knew just the person for the task.

But for now he had to get back to work. There were many loose strings to be tied before he could leave for a week.

Striding from the gallery, he headed for his Lexus, then drove the inner-city streets back to his company's headquarters.

His second-in-charge, Macy, greeted him outside his office door, her long brown hair drawn back, starkly emphasizing her sleek features. "Mr. Blakely, I have some good news."

"Come through." Damon had first employed Macy for her outstanding business skills. But he'd since discovered her thinking and strategizing was eerily similar to his, making her indispensable.

They walked through and Macy closed the door behind them. Damon rounded the desk, taking off his jacket and letting it hang on the back of his executive chair before sitting.

Macy stepped forward and handed him a report. "We've secured another of Travis Blakely's companies, Melbourne Brewing Limited."

Damon allowed himself a self-satisfied smile as he skimmed the report. "Good. He doesn't know about this one, either?"

"No, I bought the loan he'd taken out using MBL as collateral. Another one he'd taken without informing his attorneys."

Damon let his eyes drift closed to savor the rush. Revenge was oh, so sweet. He couldn't wait for the day he told his evil excuse for an uncle that he'd bought all his assets out from under him. He'd vowed as a thirteen-year-old—black, blue and bleeding from being "disciplined" by his uncle's fists—that this would come.

Damon already held the deeds to the old man's house—again Travis had used it as collateral on a loan to cover a business deal gone wrong. Damon simply bought the company that had given the loan.

Travis's main mistake had been in growing arrogant, in letting his ego make business moves his bank balance couldn't match. And Damon had been more than willing to cash in on that slip.

Though, Damon had used other tactics where needed. He'd acquired the mansion's private gallery in a deal brokered by his man on the inside. Travis thought he was selling two paintings but instead had signed over the entire gallery for a song—all because he'd assigned the task to an employee whose loyalty Damon had bought for an absurdly high price.

He knew Travis was only aware of losing two companies, ones where hostile takeovers had been necessary. And even with those, Damon had covered his tracks well enough by using companies within companies, so the only people who knew he was at the top of the chain were the two people in his office.

He spared his 2IC an approving nod. "Good work. You'll be getting a bonus."

Macy barely acknowledged the boon as she slid gracefully into the chair across from his. "That makes twenty-three companies you've acquired from Travis."

He threw the papers onto his desk and loosened his tie, righteous victory filling his chest. "Only five to go." So close now.

Macy retrieved the report, running a finger down a table of figures as if committing them to memory. "The most well-protected five, including—"

"Including BlakeCorp." He finished her sentence, stomach clenched. "I have a backup plan. You got my memo that I'll be out of the office next week?"

Macy nodded. "Do you need me to accompany you?"

"Not this time. I need you here, running things. I'll be unavailable some of the time—it's not strictly company business." A vision with silver-blond hair rose unbidden and he allowed himself a moment of appreciation before tamping down on it.

Macy arched a brow and he knew what she was thinking. He was never away from the office for anything but work.

He smiled. "Oh, I'll be working on our objectives— I'll be putting plan B into place in case we don't get the last five companies in time."

Macy's eyebrows drew together creating a tiny frown line between them. "I know I've said this before, but I'm not confident we'll be able to get those last five. Especially BlakeCorp."

Deep down, neither was Damon. In fact, the task was close to impossible. But he wouldn't stop before he owned it all. His pride demanded he take everything away from the uncle who'd treated a small child so shamefully, who hadn't honored his dead brother's wishes. That included Travis Blakely's portfolio of assets, every last coin of his cash reserves, his home, his reputation…everything. He didn't want to merely win, he wanted to see Travis destroyed, utterly and completely.

He sank back into his chair, seeing Lily's delicate beauty again in his mind. Her pure heart could never understand his black motives in his campaign against Travis. Wouldn't understand the darkness that lived inside him every waking moment.

But now that Lily was pregnant with his child, by God he'd make it a real marriage.

Everyone wore masks of one type or another. He just had to ensure his stayed firmly in place.

Three

Three days later, Lily watched from her kitchen window, a bowl of fruit salad in her hand, as Damon pulled his Lexus to the curb in front of her rented house.

He slid out and her breath caught. His khaki pants and moss-green polo shirt should have looked casual, but with the pants' crisp crease down the front and the shirt tucked in above a simple belt that had probably cost the equivalent to a month of her wages, he somehow appeared ready to lead a board meeting. Or seduce a woman.

She almost choked on her strawberry as the thought took hold and irresistible desire stole over her. The familiar luscious heat started low in her belly.

Determined not to lose control of her body, she carefully set down the bowl and gripped the edges of the sink. She would not get distracted by something as counterproductive as sexual attraction. To do the best for her baby she needed to be focused—and she would be.

She glanced out the window again and watched as Damon, folded papers in one hand, set his keyless lock and strode to her front door.

Lily took a deep breath and dried her hands to let him in. But instead of pressing the buzzer, he took out the key she'd given him while they'd dated and let himself in. Her heart twisted at the familiarity of the action, for the memories of naive happiness it evoked.

She'd asked for that key back; he'd told her he'd get around to it, but she'd known he had no intention. She guessed his reasons had something to do with a bruised sense of entitlement. She'd had every intention of changing the lock. Then she'd suspected she was pregnant, one of her assistants on the Impressionist exhibition was reassigned, and then… Well, then Travis had fallen ill and Damon had asked her to marry him.

"Lily, it's me," he called from the hall.

"I'm in the kitchen," she called back, picking up her bowl again and perching on a kitchen stool, elbows resting on the polished wood counter. He could see himself through the house—she didn't want to seem too eager and reinforce his view of their relationship.

Damon appeared in the doorway and propped one shoulder against the frame, his casual pose belying the heat in his eyes. Every cell and molecule in her body went on instant alert and every drop of hormone screamed her need for him. For all the heat and pleasure that his gaze promised.

Focus. Her chin kicked up. There were more important priorities than physical want. Like her future. And her baby's future.

He chuckled, slow and deep. "They'll feed us on the plane."

Her grasp on self-control almost wavered as his sensual rumble resonated through her, but she staved off the threat by concentrating on his words alone. "I know, but I'm pregnant and I'm hungry. This will tide me over until we board."

Broad shoulders straightened as his amusement evaporated. "Lily, you're not on your own in this. If you're hungry anytime, anywhere, tell me and I'll get what you need."

Her breathing hitched, but she wouldn't be swept away by his words. She was more than capable of feeding herself. "Thanks, but I've got some cookies in my bag. I'll be fine."

He took a step closer, his voice deepening. "I don't just mean now. I'm serious. You're carrying my baby, so you tell me whatever it is you want and I'll find it. I don't care if we're in the middle of a traffic jam or on a snowbound mountain. I'll arrange it."

His gaze was unwavering, resolute. He meant it. Well, for now. His promises only lasted until work called, but her pulse fluttered nevertheless. In this moment, he was here, looking after her, and he'd never been more attractive.

"Thank you," she whispered. She took a piece of cantaloupe and chewed carefully, desperate to do something to shield her overwhelming yearning for the man before her. She forced her gaze down to her fruit.

A silence followed and the tension escalated despite her resolve not to look up. She could feel his eyes on her—her skin prickled with heat wherever they landed. Still, she would not look.

She knew she'd have to eventually—they were getting married. At some point she'd have to face what he did to her and find a way to handle it. But for the life of her, right this minute, she couldn't think how.

Then, from the corner of her eye, she saw him open the folded papers and lay them out flat on the counter beside her.

"The bank account for the baby in your name, as requested. I've deposited an amount my lawyers tell me should be enough to support a child until he's eighteen. I didn't want you to be worried that I'll stop payments. I'll still add more at regular intervals."

Lily stopped chewing as her eyes rested on the very generous value of the account. Her mind stilled, then clicked into gear. She hadn't expected this move precisely but, knowing Damon, she had been waiting for a counteroffensive ever since she laid out her conditions. And here it was.

He'd arranged the lump sum in the bank account so there would be no need for a contract to ensure his payments. Money in the bank equaled no contract to get money. His first step in a plan to avoid signing anything pertaining to her other condition—separate bedrooms, separate lives.

Her shoulders slumped. She should have guessed he'd fight on that one. Damon always held tight to what was his.

She rubbed little circles on her temples, attempting to relieve the building pressure.

The very fact that he was manipulating her now reinforced her decision that their child couldn't grow up in the mold of the Blakelys. It would be too cruel to let an innocent baby learn the Blakely cynicism and how to bow down at the altar of the almighty dollar.

Damon played to win. At any cost. Their relationship had already been chalked up as one of those costs and she'd vowed to never give him the chance to treat her heart as expendable again. Or her baby's precious heart.

She opened her mouth to speak again, but he cut her off. "Are your bags packed? I'll take them out."

She folded her hands on the counter and squeezed them until her knuckles turned white. She needed to be strong or he'd walk all over her. She'd told him her conditions; she just had to stick to her guns and not let him manipulate her. "Damon, you haven't given me a contract yet."

He didn't flicker an eyelash. "Contract? I've already given you the money. It's the independence you wanted."

Attempting to put herself in a less submissive position, she stood. It wasn't much of an improvement, given his massive presence, but she could only work with what she had. He stood on the other side of the counter, leaning against it with one hip as if there was nothing she could say that would worry him.

She lifted her chin. "I want separate bedrooms on opposite sides of the house. I'm not saying the vows without a contract ensuring that."

Damon smiled. Her threat appeared to amuse him. He prowled around the counter and came to a stop mere inches from her.

"Sweetheart," he drawled, voice low and hypnotic, "I'm not signing my marital rights away. If you're so sure we can't live together, perhaps you should consider a different contract. Leave me sole custody."

Her hands instinctively flew to her waist. His eyes held hers. He may have been amused but he wasn't joking. She felt sick to the pit of her stomach and struggled to make her voice work. "The courts won't be swayed by your money, Damon. Or by a man who can't keep his word—you promised you'd sign the contract."

His gaze roamed to her hair and his hand reached up to run down its length, from crown to where the ends lay on her shoulder. She flinched and yet still felt compelled to lean into him. She hated herself for that weakness.

He didn't retract his hand, instead lingering over the exposed skin at the curve of her neck. "Actually, I didn't agree to sign anything."

His hands began to work their magic, sending ripples of heat and pleasure out from the spot his fingers caressed, along each and every nerve ending, all the way to her toes. As a distraction, it was effective—she paused instead of responding.

Pressing his advantage, Damon closed the last gap between them and used his other hand to press the small of her back so she leaned into him.

"Now we need to be reasonable," he breathed into her ear. "I've given you more money than most people see in their lifetime. You need this marriage as much as I do. I'm assuming you've already told your grandmother about the new house?"

Lily swallowed with difficulty and nodded.

Without her noticing, he'd maneuvered her around so her back was against the counter and she was trapped between it and the muscled wall of his chest. She could feel him against her skin, feel him *under* her skin. He'd invaded her blood and it pumped for him through her body, powerful, dark, spellbinding. As if every strong beat in her chest was his name.

He brushed his lips along her earlobe and she felt the words on his breath as much as heard them. "And yet you're willing to risk that over an unwinnable point."

She dropped her chin, only barely stifling a moan. She couldn't think. Couldn't make a thought form that didn't involve his body.

It had always been this way between them, simmering passion that ignited with a simple touch from their first kiss. Before, even—from the first time their gazes had connected at the gallery fund-raiser. Damon had prowled over, offered her a champagne flute he'd acquired on the way and asked, "How high a donation for a private tour of the gallery with—" he checked her name badge "—an assistant curator?" He'd kissed her before they made it halfway through the Australian Colonial Art exhibit.

And now he was doing it again—skipping preliminaries and rushing straight to the passion she could barely resist. If only he'd stop crowding her! She needed to step away, but there was nowhere to go. She placed her hands firmly on his shirt and pushed. He stepped back several inches, that same amused smile on his perfect mouth.

She had to focus. He was trying to take all her bargaining power away, but she wouldn't let him forget…he needed her. "You won't get BlakeCorp without me."

He raised his brows in innocent surprise. "You think I'd choose a business over a child of my own flesh and blood?" He ran a knuckle lightly down her cheek. "Lily, why make this harder than it needs to be? No one gets everything they want at a negotiation table. That's why it's called negotiation. You played your hand well and you're getting a good outcome—the bank account and your gran taken care of for the rest of her life. And me."

Him? Her whole body flushed, but she needed to stay on her game or he'd outplay her. "Damon, whether you sign a contract or not, I won't be the kind of wife you want."

"And what kind is that?" He turned slightly to lean back against the counter, ankles crossed, and thrust his hands deep into his pockets. His earlier amusement had returned.

She narrowed her eyes, wanting him to understand how serious she was about this. "I won't sleep with you."

Gran always said, start as you mean to go on. This was a marriage on paper for the sake of a will. It was not now, nor would it ever be a real marriage. She couldn't let the lines blur—not even once. Her heart was having enough trouble resisting falling in love with him again as it was. Sleeping with him would court disaster.

"Let's just say the negotiations will be ongoing on that point." He raised one brow and her stomach fell. He still intended seducing her.

Then another thought struck. "You have booked separate bedrooms wherever we're staying, haven't you?"

It'd be just like Damon to expect her to share his bed despite the boundaries she'd laid. He probably had some ridiculous excuse ready like, just because they shared a bed didn't mean they had to make love.

Though separate bedrooms might not be much of a defense when it came down to it....

He nodded, poker-faced. "As a matter of fact, I have."

"So you won't mind if I check that?" She knew how he worked and it wasn't necessarily honorable, not when he wanted something as badly as he wanted this.

A lazy grin spread across his face. "Not at all." He reached into his back pocket, withdrew his wallet and found a slip of paper that he handed her. It had a hotel name and phone number. Had he really done what she'd requested or was this another bluff?

She folded the note and stuffed it in her handbag on the bench. She'd ring to make sure when she got a private moment. When he wasn't breathing down her neck, making her lose her thoughts.

He looked around as if that was settled. "Where are your bags?"

She blinked, tried to get her bearings, and glanced down the hall. "At my bedroom door."

Lily watched him stride away, an edge of panic creeping up to clutch her chest. She had a strong feeling that she'd jumped out of the frying pan and into a bushfire.

Damon inserted the Auckland hotel room key card into the honeymoon suite's lock and turned to appraise his new wife. How would she react to being carried over the threshold? Not well, if her mood during their vows was any indication.

Her frame of mind notwithstanding, she'd looked like a vision from heaven in the Peace Chapel. And the sharp constriction of his chest had almost blindsided him. It was *right*, this union.

He'd bought her a small bouquet of lily of the valley and she'd clutched it tightly, her gaze resting on the blooms during most of the ceremony.

Her downcast eyes only added to her resemblance to the aged paintings of holy women housed in his childhood home. She'd been ethereal.

She still was as she stood motionless, waiting for him to turn the door handle.

Normally he'd be willing to risk her wrath and just sweep her into his arms to enter the room, but he had a lot riding on her mood tonight. Plans they'd both enjoy if she'd only relax.

He presented his arms. "How would you like to enter, Mrs. Blakely?"

Lily's forest-green eyes flickered with pain before landing on contempt. "I've told you, we don't have that type of marriage, Damon."

He looked her lush frame up and down. Then why had she worn white? The cotton summer dress may not look much like a traditional wedding gown, but she couldn't fool him—her sentimental streak had chosen the color as intentionally as he'd chosen her bouquet.

She could deny it all she liked, but her selection proved that deep down she acknowledged the validity of their marriage. Which gave his libido hope that the wedding night would turn out to be as traditional as the color of her dress.

He smiled at his bride as she waited for him to open the door. No doubt about it, the sentimental streak that had chosen her white attire would like to be carried over the threshold. And damn if he didn't relish the prospect himself.

He reinserted the key card to activate the lock, then leaned down and scooped her up in one smooth motion, carrying her through the door into a room elegantly decorated in whites and creams, and kicked it closed behind him.

He was pleasantly surprised she didn't object. She'd probably convince herself later it was due to shock. No matter, for now he'd savor the moment.

The scent of wildflowers enveloped him, the pressure of her body against his consumed him and he paused to let his eyes drift closed and fully appreciate the feeling.

She was tall, yet so delicate he'd often thought of her as a snow lily come to life—willowy, as if seeking the sun. He raised his lids to look his fill. Her fairness—creamy skin and silver-blond hair—only enhanced the illusion. Her eyes, the color of untamed foliage, showed where she truly belonged. Her natural habitat wasn't the art galleries her work kept her in, but where the wild lilies grew.

"Very nice, Damon. Now put me down." One side of his mouth curved at her hundred-percent controlled tone, but he sensed she was close to breaking point. He released her legs first, then, holding her torso with both hands, let her slide the way down.

His blood heated both at the sensation and at the memories it evoked. Of them making love through the night. The slide of nakedness. Of the sound deep in her throat when he touched her the ways she liked. His groin flexed and reported for duty.

By the time her feet touched the plush cream carpet strewn with rose petals, her pupils had dilated. Her breathing held an edge of raggedness.

He didn't release her. "You thinking along the same lines as me, sweetheart?"

There was a certain satisfaction in being able to call her that again. It suited her so completely, as if the term had been created for her alone. And he was sure he saw a flash of approval in her features every time it passed his lips.

She arched a brow. "I'm hoping against hope this is still the suite with two bedrooms. How's that compare to your thoughts?" She pushed against his chest and moved away. "I rang ahead to check from the airport but I've learned to never assume anything with you."

He almost laughed, but caught himself in time. Smart girl. He'd changed the arrangements only as they waited outside the chapel, predicting she'd check the hotel number he gave her before then.

He adopted an innocent air. "In a honeymoon suite?" He looked pointedly from white walls and Austrian blinds, across to a table of palest pink marble with two white lacquered chairs, to the complimentary champagne waiting in an ice bucket. "Can't imagine how likely that option would be."

Her jaw dropped and her mouth formed a perfect

little O. Then her fists clenched at her sides. "This is *not* a honeymoon. It's a contractual agreement."

He grinned. "Language can be so confining. Let's just wait and see exactly what we have here."

She shook her head as if words failed her. Then he watched, enjoying her profile as she bent to unzip her suitcase, left neatly beside his on matching luggage stands by hotel staff. Her sweet upturned nose, lush pink lips, just begging…

"If you think I'm sharing a bed with you, then you haven't remembered me properly." She straightened, lemon silky robe and pajamas over one arm, the other planted firmly on her hip.

Oh, he remembered all right. Remembered she liked to think she was in control. And sometimes he let her. Then, when she'd stopped fighting, he'd convince her of his point in other ways. Oh, yes, he remembered some very pleasant convincing.

She rubbed a hand over her eyes and leaned a little unsteadily onto the wall beside her. "I need a long, hot shower. And when I come out I expect you'll have arranged separate beds." As she lowered her hand from her face, he was shocked to see her now-lackluster complexion.

His stomach fell and all thoughts of passion evaporated. "Something's wrong. Is it the baby?" Maybe he'd pushed her too fast in her condition? Despite getting the all clear from three doctors for the flights, had it been too much for her to fly while pregnant?

He moved to her side and encircled her in his arms. The health of the tiny life she carried was the one thing they were in complete agreement on. He needed this baby—his plan B. But it was more than that. Something personal between him and the child that he couldn't yet define. A connection, a link.

She twisted to move from his embrace. "Nothing's wrong with the baby. I'm just tired from the rush to pack and the flight."

This time he didn't let her go. Instead, he guided her to the cream, overstuffed couch. "Sit down for a few minutes."

When she opened her mouth to disagree, he laid a finger across her lips. "Just this once, do something I suggest without arguing. Rest before getting in the shower. I don't want you fainting in there." He arched an eyebrow.

Her eyes widened as she took his meaning—either sit with him for a moment or risk having him checking on her, naked and wet in the shower stall. A job so appealing his temperature nudged up a couple of degrees just thinking about it.

With innate grace, she sank into the luxurious couch and rested the side of her face on the high headrest. He had to remember she was almost four months pregnant. Easy to forget when she showed so few signs, but he'd thought about the situation a lot since the night she'd sprung the news on him.

And in a surprise to himself, he'd grown more fascinated by the idea she was carrying his child inside her. Moved, even. When he'd devised this plan after his uncle's offer, he hadn't stopped to think of the emotional bond he'd feel to the baby. After his disastrous childhood, he'd have been happy going through life never reproducing.

And yet…even now, there was a tiny version of him under Lily's hands as they rested on her belly. Where did the baby fit? Lily may be tall, but she was slim. In fact, she could use a bit more meat on her bones. He'd start working on that from today, too. This woman was carrying his child and he'd make damn sure both of them had everything they needed.

"Tell me what you know about the baby." He hadn't finished forming the thought before it was out of his mouth.

Her eyes opened slowly, lazily, and she smiled. "I don't know much yet. No gender. But everything is progressing as it should be for this far along."

Damon grabbed on to the small morsel of information, yet still needing more. "Can you…" He cleared his throat. "Can you feel him move?"

"Not yet. Sometime in the next couple of weeks, the experts say."

Sitting there on the couch, hands clasped over their child, lashes fluttering to rest on her cheeks, she was so damn beautiful, the epitome of what a mother should be—soft, protective, kind. Despite his threat in her kitchen about giving him sole custody, he'd never act on it. Having been deprived of a mother's love for most of his childhood, he knew its value.

His hand reached out, almost of its own volition, then retracted. It seemed an intimacy too far. Strange, when they were married and would be lovers again as soon as she stopped fighting it. And this was *his* baby.

Yet something still kept him from forcing this intrusion on her without invitation. Something about her now, perhaps the glow radiating from her skin, which made her look like the Madonna portrait that had hung in his childhood schoolroom.

She was high above him, he with his blackened heart. He was under no illusions about the darkness that consumed him inside, a consequence of being raised by an instrument of the devil. A man who had no boundaries on the methods he used—even on a child. Cruelty, humiliation, violence, thievery.

Damon had always prided himself that no matter how low he sank, he never stooped as low as Travis. But now, looking down on Lily, untainted by darkness, he could see his own true colors.

God knew, it was too late for him. The only way to save himself now was to have her purity beside him, part of him. She'd give him an heir, BlakeCorp and personal salvation.

He needed to have her, now more than ever.

Decision made beyond question, he smiled, using all his charm. "The color's returned to your cheeks. You look well enough for that shower now. I'll order up some food while you're in there."

Her eyes drifted open, a cool green gaze landed on his for a moment, lingered, then she turned away and nodded.

Unsettled but determined, he watched her go and made a vow to himself.

He would have her. Tonight.

Four

Lily lay across the bed in the dusk-darkened room. She stretched, feeling the slide of her satin pajamas on her skin, listening to the shower running, knowing Damon was in there, soapy, warm and beautiful. The open-plan room design only made things worse—no lock separated them, he stood just out of sight, literally around a white-tiled corner.

And he knew it, had planned it this way.

Being this close was playing havoc with her mind and body, and he knew that, too. Wherever she was, part of her focus always seemed to be reminiscing about their lovemaking, trying to block those memories, or wondering about making new memories....

She could walk into that bathroom now, drop her pajamas and robe and slip into the shower. He'd welcome her, pull her close under the spray, perhaps languidly soap her up, running a hand over her glistening skin, and she'd slide her tongue along his strong jaw, down his throat, then—

No. She groaned as she faced away from that side of the suite and dragged herself back from the brink. That would only increase her involvement—and more than instinct told her she was too deep already. She *couldn't* fall in love with him again. It almost destroyed her last time. Never again would she fall for a man as self-serving, morally bankrupt, and as much of a workaholic as Damon Blakely.

She sighed and slid a glance toward the bathroom. Of course, she had to admit she loved the way he looked at her as if she were a rare delicacy. Loved the way he walked into a room and his presence instantly dominated it. Loved his troubled heart that he kept so guarded and hidden, even from himself. Loved the way his skin felt under her hands, under her mouth.

But, regardless of whether her heart remained intact this time or not, she knew one thing for sure: contrary to popular wisdom, love was not nearly enough.

Her mother had loved her father and the results had been devastating, for both of them and for her, their only child. She'd been notified a week after her fifteenth birthday that they'd died in a road accident. They said her mother fell asleep at the wheel and ran off the road.

Lily's hand went to her mother's silver heart pendant hanging on a fine silver chain around her neck. It was the sum total of her inheritance from her parents—the only item of value in their possessions.

She gripped the silver heart tighter as she wondered again if her mother had reached breaking point and seen no other way out. She'd cried for them and herself, but had been grateful they'd sent her to live with Gran three years earlier.

Supposedly the change had been to give her a chance to stay in one place, but Lily had always known that her grandmother had demanded she be sent to her. Her parents, like two kids on an adventure, lacked the will to disobey Gran, whose own backbone was pure steel. Lily had been offered occasional sympathy over the years as the girl given up by her parents. But even at twelve Lily had seen the situation clearly—Gran had rescued her and Lily would be forever grateful.

The years with her parents had been unpredictable and confusing, and had left her craving stability. They said one thing but meant another. Their well-meaning inconsistency was one of the reasons she understood the way Damon's mind worked. He'd promise her the world, but he always ended up getting what he wanted.

Words were easy for her parents, for Damon. Actions told the real story. Damon's priorities were the only ones that mattered to him.

She would never live that way again—it was soul-destroying to feel valueless.

More important, she would save her baby from that environment. Already, she loved this tiny person too much to subject it to the emotional torment a life with Damon would surely bring.

The water stopped and she sat bolt upright, listening to the sounds of Damon moving about in the bathroom.

A cold sweat broke out over her skin. The man in the bathroom was her *husband*. The thought hit her with sickening force. She'd gone through with it. She'd married Damon Blakely. They'd exchanged vows of love, fidelity and commitment. Vows neither of them intended to honor.

Jitters all the way to her fingers and toes replaced her fatigue. She'd really done it.

A knock on the door interrupted her thoughts.

"Room service." The call made her stomach rumble. How long since she'd eaten? Too long. She stood and padded out to open the door.

Three men in maroon-and-gold uniforms stood waiting behind multilayered trolleys. Lily's jaw dropped. What in the name of heaven was this? There must be enough food here to feed the entire floor! She stood back to let them pass.

The first two men pushed their deliveries past her, parked their trolleys beside the pale pink marble table and began laying out linen and cutlery. The third man gave her a slight bow on the way past and left his trolley a little behind the others.

"Dessert," he said, looking at her and then at a spot over her shoulder.

Lily turned to see Damon coming through the bedroom doorway, tying the sash on the large white hotel bathrobe that draped his frame, midnight hair damp, feet bare on the thick carpet. She remembered how her hands followed the trail of hair down his chest, hard stomach and lower. Dizzy with lust, she could do no more than lick her dry lips.

How would she resist this man if, *when,* he made that inevitable concerted effort to seduce her? He would try and she must resist no matter how much she craved his touch. It would be difficult, if not impossible, to re-establish her ground rules after they made love even once. She had to remember that he had an ulterior motive. She was his ticket to BlakeCorp.

"Ah, the food's arrived." His voice was a low rumble that soaked in and touched her deep in her bones.

Damon reached into the robe's pocket and withdrew several folded notes, which he gave to the men in turn. The first two bowed and left the room; the third looked down at the tip and grinned. "Thanks, Mr. Blakely."

Damon closed the door behind them, then leaned back against it, a hungry smile stretching his features. But his eyes were on her, not the food.

An answering quiver raced through her body. She couldn't let the false intimacy created by their paper marriage alter her decision to not sleep with him. And from the look on his face, he would turn every inch she gave him into a mile and then some.

Trembling, she turned back to the food, fussing with the place settings with unmanageable fingers.

"No need to be scared of me, sweetheart." She imagined—*felt*—him walking up behind her. When he spoke next, he was right behind her, his breath lifting the sensitive hairs by her ear. "I'm not the big bad wolf."

Oh, how wrong he was.

The heat from his body seeped into hers, turning her bones to warm honey. If only their relationship was unfettered—as it'd been before the will, before her pregnancy, before he'd broken her heart—she would be free to lean back into him and take what he offered. The pleasures he could bestow went beyond anything she expected to experience again. She shuddered with the desire her body remembered too clearly. If only she could have just one more sample—

As if reading her thoughts, Damon placed a butterfly kiss behind her ear, sending a delicious shiver across her skin. Then another kiss and another shiver. She opened her mouth, knowing she should protest, but before she could speak, he nipped at her earlobe and sucked it into the decadent heat of his mouth.

Lily stifled a groan, almost lost, barely able to form the thought that she should move away, but his warm breath rippled sideward to her cheekbone, and she caught the fragrance of toothpaste—fresh mint mingling with his own scent.

"God, what you do to me," he whispered.

What she did to *him?* Within short minutes of his ministrations she was ready to fly to the moon with him. She leaned back against his body, desperate to learn he was as affected as her. Just for a moment, she told herself. And, oh, he was. His arousal pushed against the small of her back.

"Damon, I—"

He raised a finger and placed it over her lips but it did more than silence her. The pad of his finger traced a leisurely path across her bottom lip before dipping into her mouth. Breathing choppy, body aflame, she welcomed the finger, closed her lips around it, sucked ever so lightly, intensifying the mounting tension pulling at her core.

Light-headed, she grasped for his arm in an attempt to steady herself so as not to miss a single delicious moment.

He swore under his breath then slowly withdrew the finger and placed a chaste kiss on the top of her head. "First things first," he rasped before clearing his throat. "I need to feed you." He took her elbow and guided her to one of the ornate white lacquered chairs. "Sit."

The room slanted at his change of direction but she sank down and let Damon push her chair in, trying to counter her disorientation. How had that happened? She bit down on her lip. Thank heaven now she had time to rebuild her defenses—make them impenetrable.

He sat in his own chair, toweling robe displaying a proud V of solid chest dusted with hair, golden forearms peeking out his rolled-back sleeves letting her see their muscles contract and flex as he lifted the lid off the first dish. The spicy aroma filled her senses and she reluctantly dragged her gaze from Damon to the food, still a touch dizzy.

"I ordered a selection. This one's Asian stir-fry vegetables." He held out his hand for her plate. She complied, realizing how hungry she was, and not just for Damon, then took the plate back after he'd spooned a portion onto it.

After scooping vegetables onto his own plate, he lifted the second lid revealing a cheesy topping covering something enticing underneath.

Again he held his hand for her plate. "I ordered the three dishes on the menu with cheese—you need calcium. But I made sure there was none of the soft cheese you can't have while pregnant." He looked up, one corner of his mouth curved in a lazy grin when he saw her surprise. "I've done some research."

Touched that he'd given so much thought to the ordering, she watched as he lifted lid after lid, working through the dishes he'd ordered for her. A lump grew to fill her throat.

By the time he came to the sixth dish, her plate was piled so high it resembled more a small mountain than dinner.

She laughed and threw up her hands. "That's enough. I'll never be able to eat all of this."

He nodded and continued piling new dishes onto his plate. "Just eat what you can. You and the baby need sustenance."

She waited for him to finish serving himself before tasting. The food was divine, just like the other five-star places Damon had taken her when they'd dated. But more than the food affected her.

Watching Damon eat, dressed only in a bathrobe, kept her blood simmering and her senses on high alert. The robe's wide gap at his chest gave her an unobstructed view of his strong, cleanly shaven throat, Adam's apple bobbing as he swallowed.

He held out his fork to her. "Try this. It's one you don't have."

Lily hesitated, breath catching in her chest. He'd fed her from his fork before, and occasionally from his fingers, like the night he'd fed her mango slices in bed. The memory of the sensual delights that night had brought dropped her mouth open and she accepted his fork.

The light-as-air pumpkin soufflé melted on her tongue.

"Mmm, fabulous." Her eyes drifted closed to make the most of the flavor, licking her lips for any remnants.

"I'll tell you what's fabulous," Damon said in a husky voice. "That licking noise you're making. Here, try this one."

Her eyes flew open as she realized how it must look from his position. She felt the blush creep up her neck. "Ah, no thanks. I have enough here." It wasn't fair to tease him, lead him on, when she had no intention of sleeping with him. Heaven knew, she certainly shouldn't have let him kiss her ear earlier. Her guard had to stay in place.

Then again, a voice taunted in her mind, Damon never needed encouragement. He always knew what he wanted and right now he wanted her.

"Well, let me try some of yours. I didn't get any of that creamy cheese dish," he said, pointing to the side of her plate. "I left it in case you wanted seconds." His lips sat parted for a second before he added, "Just a taste."

The rasp in his voice called to her and without thinking, she lifted her fork to his mouth. She instantly regretted it when his lips clamped around her fork. He held it between his teeth, his eyes intense as they captured hers as surely as he'd captured the fork.

Then he let the clean fork slide free, chewed leisurely and swallowed. "I've dreamed of tasting you again. Your lips…your skin. Your essence."

Lily couldn't speak, could barely breathe. She was baking inside, melting, *needing* his touch. She'd never had so skilled a lover as Damon, one who so thoroughly reveled in her body and in her pleasure. What she wouldn't give to experience that again. Just for one night.

No! She flinched at the physical pain of breaking eye contact, as if she was being torn in two. It took everything she had to take another mouthful and chew, pretending she was unaffected when she was ready to combust. Damon knew her weakness for his body. She suspected he knew that any woman would have a weakness for his skills once they'd experienced them. And one thing she knew about her new husband—he wouldn't hesitate to use any means at his disposal to get what he wanted.

And what he wanted was his father's company…and that meant keeping her with him until their baby was born so it would be legitimate. He'd use any means at his disposal—including seduction—to keep her in the marriage until then. Her heart clutched tight. She must be strong. Not put one night's passion ahead of her baby's needs, or she'd risk her child's future, the chance for her baby to have a stable and secure childhood—something that meant more to her than anything.

On autopilot, she kept eating—food on her fork, chew, swallow, repeat. With nerves jangling, the taste of the dishes no longer registered; all she was aware of was the man across from her. Without looking, she knew he watched her, could feel his gaze as a physical touch.

"You seem tense." His voice was so low it was almost a growl.

She didn't answer. Instead, she focused on her food, the only hunger she could safely assuage.

With slow, deliberate movements, Damon stood and moved behind her chair. "I can help with that tension in your shoulders." His hands gently kneaded her shoulders, and his heat seeped through her satin pajamas and robe as if he'd touched her bare skin.

She twisted away. "Damon, we've talked about—"

He maneuvered her back against the chair and cut off her words. "It's not the time for talking."

His fingers massaged deeply, with wonderful pressure and sensuous movements, spreading heat across her tired muscles. The relaxing rhythm of his hands through the slippery material lulled her into a place of mindless, sensual bliss. No one had touched her this way since…Damon. Her body, starved for warmth, soaked up his attention.

His newly shaven jaw scraped deliciously over her ear. "Better?"

His voice flowed across her skin. Perhaps just a moment longer. She tilted her head forward. She was so tired, her muscles were in knots, and Damon's hands were oh, so skilled. Might as well enjoy the massage he offered. She sighed and relaxed back into the intoxicating familiarity of him.

"Better," she relented on a sigh.

He reached around and loosened her robe then, slipping his fingers beneath the collar, he let it fall from her shoulders. Consumed by his touch, she couldn't find the wherewithal to even protest; only a distant part of her mind warned that she was inviting trouble. Inviting bliss. He parted her silky top a little and dipped his hands inside to keep rubbing her shoulders, skin on skin.

"Your muscles are so tight. You need to relax." His voice was easy, as soothing as a friend advising a friend—a well-timed tactic, she knew. He confined his hands to her shoulders, but this was more than a platonic massage, it always was with his touch. Her breasts tightened, their tips aching for his caress, and a dull throb pulsated at her core. Against her better judgment, her body was responding to his.

"Let go of all that tension you're holding, Lily." This time his voice dropped to a seductive whisper. Totally absorbed in the exquisite sensations, she let her chin fall to her chest. A small moan escaped her throat.

"Just relax." She felt his hands joined by his hot, wet mouth. He used his tongue and teeth in conjunction with his hands, amplifying the effect, dragging her deeper under his thrall.

When his hands slipped farther under her top to her breasts and ran across their tips, she almost dissolved into a pool of desire, her last remnants of self-control hanging by a frayed thread.

Yet she somehow forced the whisper out. "Damon, I'm already pregnant. We don't need to have sex." He was using her, she knew it, but his hands on her felt so good, their touch scrambled her brain.

She gasped when he cupped each breast and feathered moist kisses down the back of her neck. "If we're talking about need, don't doubt that I need you," he ground out. "What I feel when I'm near you has always been beyond want."

Lily bit her lip, her mind slowly waking to find itself at war with her body. "I don't think it's a good idea."

"We're married. We want each other." He nipped at

the spot where her neck curved into her shoulders, continuing to use his knowledge of her body against her. "The question is, why wouldn't we make love?"

Despite *knowing* a reason existed, with his tongue tracing circles on her shoulder blade and his hands on her breasts, she struggled to come up with her name let alone an answer.

Then his hands reached around, loosened the sash of her satin robe and any last vestiges of her earlier resolve evaporated. A moan ripped from her throat. She turned in her chair and sought his lips; she'd deal with the fallout in the morning. Forget forever. This was about here, now, tonight.

Damon needed no urging. His mouth claimed hers with the same hunger threatening to consume her whole. Without breaking their kiss, he circled around and came to kneel in front of her, between her parted knees, his hands holding her face.

Pushing his thick toweling robe to the edge of his broad shoulders, she ran her fingers over his back, luxuriating in the feel of his skin. Smooth and warm under her hands. God above, how she'd missed the feel of his skin against her body. Starving for him, she pushed the robe farther down, leaving the vast expanse of his back and shoulders free to her touch. The smell of clean, naked man—and not just any man, *her* man—made her light-headed with desire.

"Lily," he groaned and pulled back a little so she could see the emotion in his ice-blue eyes. "It's never been like this with anyone else."

He sank back into her, the wall of his chest pressed

against her breasts, as he whispered against her mouth, "Only you."

Not wanting to waste a moment on analysis, she opened her mouth to him, needing him more than she'd ever needed anyone.

"One of us is overdressed," he murmured. Deftly, he removed her robe, pushing it down her arms to pool behind her on the chair, not breaking the kiss for a second.

"Layers." Damon grinned as his fingers worked the buttons of her pajama top free. "Like playing pass the parcel as a kid." Undoing the last one, he opened the sides. "Except I don't have to share the prize."

He dipped his head and took one nipple in his mouth. Her lips parted under his exacting persuasion and she melted, hands drawn to his head, repeating his name, "Damon."

She imagined his hardness twitching between his thighs, down too low for her to feel, and she wanted more, God help her, wanted everything all at once. Yet part of her had to make sure he understood her position. She dragged his face back to hers.

"Damon," she gasped between desperately snatched kisses. "This doesn't set a precedent."

He grinned around her lips. "I understand."

Was that agreement? He nipped at her bottom lip and her train of thought began to disappear, yet she clung to it. She needed to have this clear before giving herself permission to enjoy him fully. "It's just this once?"

His mouth trailed across her cheek then he whispered with heated breath in her ear. "Whatever you say."

For now that had to be enough. She let herself go,

turning to him and kissing him with everything she had. "Now, please," she begged.

He pulled away. "Not a chance. I've been dreaming about being here with you for months. I'm taking my time." He gave her a slow, sensual smile full of promise and dipped farther this time, to her stomach.

Lily closed her eyes, feeling his tongue flick out and scald just below a breast, then teeth nipping on her side. His mouth moved across her belly, kissing a spot then sucking the skin in through his teeth. She writhed below him, the pleasure-pain a beautiful torture. When he released the skin, he blew on the spot and somewhere in the back of her mind she understood he'd marked her stomach. Claimed her and their baby.

Then he moved lower still and her mind went utterly blank. He pulled her silken pajamas down with hands that moved an inch ahead of his mouth, then tossed them aside.

When he reached the juncture of her thighs, he kissed her reverently, then laid his cheek against her and wrapped his arms around her hips, hugging tightly. "God, I've missed you."

The gesture and words brought tears to her eyes, but before sentiment could carry her away, he turned his face and raised one of her knees then the other over his shoulders. She shivered with anticipation, knowing of his sixth sense for lovemaking—he understood her body and its needs better than she did herself.

He slid his hands underneath her and cupped a buttock in each—lifting her to his face.

As his tongue dipped into her, little arrows of

pleasure darted out from her core to the top of her head and tips of her toes.

He withdrew his tongue, teasing. "You've missed me, too?"

"Oh, yes." She writhed in his strong hands still holding her firmly and his tongue dipped again, this time stroking deeply, smoothly, in a rhythm that slowly drove her wild.

Needing to do something with the building energy, her feet slipped down his back to his sides and she pressed her toes into his waist, pulling him closer.

His tongue circled and flicked, raising the tension in her every muscle. She reached out to grab the back of the chair behind her, needing an anchor before she burst free of the world.

One hand moved from her hips and then there were fingers joining his mouth, caressing…probing…finding…pleasuring…

Her body tensed to the point of exquisite throbbing and she let go of the chair, searching for him, needing to touch him, finding his shoulders and digging her fingers into his solidness.

With a tidal wave of sensation, she climaxed against his mouth, calling his name, feeling their souls entwine. The rush of pure rapture touched every part of her body—an eternity of ecstasy in every moment. And even as the intensity began to ebb, the blissful pleasure remained unabated.

She came back to awareness slowly as Damon slid up her body and pulled her into his tender embrace. Ripples of paradise still spread through her body and she rested her face on the crisp hair of his chest, knowing he was right—it had never been like this with anyone else. And she couldn't imagine it ever would be.

When they made love, they made magic.

Strength seeped back into her muscles, letting her snake her arms around his torso and hug him tightly. Then, unable to resist, her hands drifted lower, over his firm buttocks, scraping her fingernails lightly there, the way he liked, then moving around to encircle him in her hand.

Ah, the feel of him. Burning hot, silky smooth.

Strong arms wrapped around her and lifted her from the chair, then laid her down on the plush carpet beside him. For a moment she hugged him tight, the sensation of his naked length against her skin feeling so *right*.

Then, unable to wait any longer, she moved down his body, just to see him again, to wrap both hands around him, to claim him with her mouth the way he'd claimed her. Her mind may have chosen to break up with Damon, but her heart and body held a different opinion on the matter. Now they were in control, she leaned in, as possessive as any bear guarding what was hers.

Holding him before her, she closed her eyes and tasted him. He groaned, then rasped, "Lily, wait."

He edged his way back the short distance to the wall and leaned his shoulders against it, sitting with his legs extended on the soft cream carpet. His golden body smattered with dark hair was posed like an erotic portrait that the artist in her appreciated as much as the wanton woman who'd emerged. She followed on all fours, unwilling to let him out of her reach.

"That's better," he said, voice slightly slurred in satisfaction as he caressed her back, then around to cup a breast. "I can reach you better."

Her pulse picked up again, from the erotic view before her and the attentions of his fingers. He stroked the pad of his thumb across a taut nipple, sending shock waves down to the flesh he'd so recently pleasured, and she took him deeper over and over again.

He was hers.

"Lily, come here." His voice was strained, perched on the brink of release.

Reluctant to leave, she waited until he called again. "Sweetheart, bring those lips up here."

Smiling recklessly, she made her way back to his decadent mouth before he slid the two of them sideways down to the floor. She could feel the length of him against her and finally, *finally,* she knew he'd soon be inside her. Spiraling out of control, unable to wait any longer, she reached to pull him on top.

He didn't budge. "Can I hurt the baby?"

"No." She pulled at him again.

He brought her closer on her side, flush against him. "Even so—" looping a hand under her knee, he pulled her leg up and around him, locking it into place "—I'll feel better this way."

Hips squared against each other as they lay on their sides, she arched back to feel him closer still. Then in one even stroke, he entered her, filling her as only he could.

She gripped his shoulders, this time knowing she was leaving marks, and tightened around him, eyes drifting closed, just reveling in this *completeness* he gave her. Warm, full lips moved on hers and she opened her mouth, welcoming the twofold connection of their bodies, the dual intimacy.

He thrust again, her name on his lips.

She met each stroke with her own push, their synchronized movements building momentum, taking her higher, back to paradise.

Her breasts felt the repeated rasp of his chest hair as his breathing became ragged and his lungs expanded to gasp more air.

She was close to the edge…hurtling toward the precipice…falling over…flying, free…floating…

And she felt Damon convulse and follow her and the feeling of completeness returned, filling every cell of her being.

Five

As he held her tightly, waiting for their breathing to return to normal, Damon felt Lily press a tender kiss to his damp chest. He allowed himself a self-satisfied smile—Lily was back in his arms, having just loved him with her body.

He'd thought he might need to work a little harder than this to claim her again. But he wouldn't look a gift horse in the mouth. They were together again. They'd soon be a family. He'd have everything he could ever want—all his uncle's assets including BlakeCorp, his baby, and pure-hearted Lily in his bed permanently. Something close to happiness filled his chest.

He held her a little tighter until she pushed him back, laughing. "I'm having enough trouble breathing as it is, Damon."

He smiled indulgently and turned onto his back, drawing her across his chest. "I'm having a little trouble getting my breath back, too."

She lifted her face and propped it onto fists resting on his chest. Her features formed a wistful expression, with what was perhaps a small cloud of doubt reflected in her eyes. "I'm glad I'm not the only one."

He met her gaze. "No question of that." He tucked her head under his chin. "It seems the question of separate bedrooms has become moot. You have the bank account but you won't be needing that room on the other side of the house anymore."

He felt her flinch then draw in a deep breath. "Yes, I do."

Her words hit him in the gut, hard and fast. What was she talking about? They'd just made love. Consummated their marriage. "You'll share my room, my bed. I'm your husband now." The father of their baby. He held her tighter. "I'll look after you."

"Damon, you're…" She shook her head and rolled off him onto her back on the soft deep carpet, looking up at the ceiling. "This can't be a proper relationship. I've already told you, I need people who are emotionally reliable." Her voice was soft, but underscored with an unswerving belief in what she'd said.

A monster swelled in his chest. He rolled on his side, needing to face this head-on. He pitched his voice low and kept absolute control over it. Rule one when threatened: control is your friend. "Whatever you thought before doesn't apply now." Hadn't he just shown her how committed he was? Hell, he'd just married her. Did she think he took that lightly?

She twisted to face him as well, biting the inside of her cheek before speaking. "Do you remember the day we broke up?"

He nodded, bringing the details to mind. "Of course."

She took a shuddering breath, then another and when she looked at him, a sheen covered her green eyes.

He reached for her, to offer comfort, to end this nowhere conversation, but she held up a hand and he dropped his arm to his side for the moment. He'd let her say her piece, then they would move on.

She spoke with quiet determination. "I rang and asked you to come out to Gran's place because I needed your financial advice. You'd said you'd help, that you'd think of a way to save her small nest egg after the market turned."

"And I came." He'd played that day over in his mind countless times and had a sinking feeling about where she was going with this. But he'd only done what needed to be done.

Her body seemed to curl in on itself, yet she held his gaze. "No, you made the journey, but as soon as you arrived you took a call and left." The anguish in her eyes was as fresh as if it'd happened yesterday.

He hated that he'd contributed to her pain, but he could only offer the truth. Surely anyone—particularly his bride—would understand. "It was a business emergency. I had no choice."

She nodded, resigned, her shoulders hunched as if defeated. "You seem to have a lot of business emergencies."

What did she want from him—blood? His options in situations like these were so limited that alternatives may as well be nonexistent. His company bought and sold other companies, specialized in hostile takeovers. Even before he'd started fleecing assets from beneath his uncle's nose, there weren't many quiet days on the job. He thought she'd understood that when he'd explained on their first date.

He exhaled. Fine. He'd take the time to explain again. He spoke gently, but firmly. "In my line of work, situations often require immediate crisis management." As it was, each twenty-four-hour period barely had space to fit in six hours of sleep and the hour at the gym he needed to keep his mind operating at the top of his game. Anything else was a luxury.

Lily wrapped her arms around herself. He frowned. Was that gooseflesh erupting over her skin? He reached for his robe and wrapped it around her like a blanket. She waited, allowing him, and didn't object when he left his hands resting on the thick terry toweling at her waist. It felt right. She obviously knew it as well as him.

She kept her eyes on his hands. "That's what it was like in my dad's so-called job. Work came first. He barely noticed anything else until he won or his money ran out." She met his gaze. "It's your choice to live that way, solely for your own needs and priorities. But it's no way to raise a child."

"Lily," he said, using his most soothing tone, "this is an overreaction about one event. I know it was less than good timing for you but—"

"It wasn't just *one* time," she interrupted, then bit

down so hard on her lip, he worried she might break the skin and draw blood. "A week before that, I rang because I needed you. We'd had news that Gran's leg required surgery."

He frowned, searching his memory. "I don't remember that."

"I know." She gave a weak smile that didn't reach her eyes. "I waited until after work hours then rang and said I needed to see you. All I wanted was your arms around me, you telling me everything would be all right. But you had a lead on stocks from a mining company you were after. You said you'd be there all night."

Irritation flared as he set his jaw, hardly able to believe she'd chosen that one night. "That was an extraordinary circumstance. That company was vitally important."

"We were only together six months, Damon, but I could give you at least five other examples. If that's how dependable and committed you are during a honeymoon phase, how would you act after five years? Or ten?"

She sat up, clutching his bathrobe tighter, letting his arm slide away. "At the beginning I thought I could handle it, but the more it happened…" She closed her eyes and shook her head as if chasing away a horrid image. Finally she took a deep breath and met his gaze again. "I couldn't live with the neglect or hurt of being dismissed as less important than work." She gulped in a mouth of air. "I'm sorry but the bottom line is…you're just not the kind of man I need."

His face burned as if she'd slapped him hard and for an instant he thought she might have. He felt his jaw clench but collected himself, waited a beat then spoke in a carefully controlled voice, barely moving a muscle. "And what kind is that?"

Her eyes filled with tears and one spilled over, creeping down her cheek. "The kind who's there for me. And my baby."

A stab of self-doubt penetrated the barrier he'd carefully built around himself over the years. But he deflected it and cleared his throat. He could handle this. Handle her. He needed to remind her of one crucial fact. "*Our* baby, Lily."

"Our baby," she conceded softly. She stood and secured the already snug-fitting robe around herself as she headed for the bathroom.

Damon scrubbed his hands through his hair. He could fix this setback. First and foremost he was a troubleshooter. A damn good one. He could gain control here with the same expertise he used in a takeover bid, ensuring he kept her and his baby. He needed a plan—a foolproof one.

A way to prove he was the *only* man she needed.

As the plane taxied down the runway two days later and leaped into the sky, Lily settled back, surrounded by her wide seat for the four-hour flight from Auckland to Melbourne.

She was so tired she could barely keep her eyes open. Was part of her fatigue from flying while pregnant? Not being a world traveler, she had no idea, but sleepless nights certainly hadn't helped.

Damon reached for her hand and interlaced their fingers. "You okay?"

Since the incredible lovemaking and the ensuing tense conversation on their wedding night, things had been exceedingly polite between them. He hadn't tried to seduce her again and for that she was grateful.

Well, mostly grateful. He'd slept on the couch both nights—including the first night after they'd made love—leaving her restless, in a heated tangle of sheets, *aching* for him. Several times she'd been at the bedroom door in a haze of need, heading for his sleeping form before she caught herself. The wrench of turning from him had been almost unbearable, but she couldn't afford to give in again—she might not have the strength to pull away as she'd already done.

So, yes, she was grateful. He was honoring her wishes; why would she undermine that? She'd created the distance between them, made her bed. Now she had to lie in it.

Though deep down she wondered if he was planning something. Damon wasn't the type to give in easily, particularly not now that he'd decided she was a necessity of life.

Perhaps politeness was his latest tactic? Lull her into a false sense of security before bringing out the heavy artillery.

She sighed. If so, there was nothing to do but wait for the show. She was simply too exhausted to even think about it now.

He was still looking at her, waiting for her reply about whether she was okay. She gave him a weary smile. "When I've had more sleep, I'll feel better."

With a conspiratorial gleam in his eye, he said,

"I've organized a few surprises to take the load off when we get back."

Heart sinking, she stifled a groan. Anything Damon thought would be a pleasant surprise was likely as not to cause more stress. She turned her head against the headrest and faced him. "What surprises?"

He squeezed her hand, still interlaced with his. "No need for concern, sweetheart. They're good things." His gaze slid over her body and he smiled. "To make your life easier."

As if cold fingers gripped her throat tightly, she couldn't speak. Had she just been thinking they had distance? And now he'd confirmed her dark suspicions—he'd been strategizing all this time. And whatever he had organized, it wasn't as innocent as he implied.

She swallowed and tried to make her throat work. "I'd rather know now." When he pressed his lips together and looked as if he wouldn't divulge any more, she added, "Don't make me worry all the way home, Damon. Please just tell me what you've organized."

He considered a moment then smiled indulgently. "I've had your furniture and belongings moved into my new house. I used an outfit my company's called in before. They go in, pack everything, move it and unpack at the other end. Your things will be exactly as you left them in your place, down to the position of your hairbrush on the dresser in our room."

Lily shook her head and tried to clear her fuzzy mind. Did he just say that strangers had handled everything she owned, including the private and personal? That, whether she'd wanted to move every last thing or not, all her belongings were now in his new house, which she'd never seen and had absolutely no links with. And that her personal belongings would be in *their* room!

A dull throb began behind her eyes and she spoke through flattened lips. "You moved my things. Without asking or even telling me?"

His brows drew together in a confused frown. "I didn't want you lifting boxes while you're pregnant, or worrying about the move. I read that stress can cause miscarriage." His eyelids dropped to half-mast, ice-blue irises determined. "I plan to make your life one hundred percent hassle-free."

She almost laughed at the irony. After all the neglect in their earlier dating life, *now* he'd decided to go to the other extreme.

The dull throb drummed and pounded. She lifted a free hand to shield her sensitive gaze from the window's light. And he wanted to reduce her worry because she was pregnant. Right. He didn't think moving her things would cause stress? Was he blind?

No—she sighed—he was just being Damon.

She shook her head and kept her voice calm. "I told you I won't share your bedroom. I've said it over and over, in fact."

He looked at her as if she needed a gentle reminder. "You were with me all the way the other night on the carpet. Whether you say the words or not, it's obvious— you want this as much as I do."

She flushed. "That was once."

"It was twice for you, if I remember correctly." Heat flared in his gaze as it roamed her face, landing on her mouth. "Even if you count it as once, it was still the best *once* of our lives. Surely you won't throw that away."

Her body tingled as he lifted their joined hands and kissed her fingertips, then her eyes were drawn as he casually shifted his long legs, the muscles of his strong thigh outlined by the fabric. An answering flame to the one she'd seen in his eyes lit inside her. She closed her eyes to douse the sensation before she lost sight of her anger at his easy dismissal of her viewpoint. Had he listened at all to what she said after they'd made love?

Suddenly she understood. He'd listened too well. Maybe this was Damon proving he could be there for her. If so, he'd missed the point. And as soon as he thought he'd convinced her, he'd return to his workaholic ways.

He stroked his thumb along the back of her hand—meant to be soothing, it was anything but to her taut nerves. "It's not complicated, Lily. We're married, expecting a baby, and we need each other—I need you to get what Travis stole from me, and you need me for the financial security you've always wanted. Besides, even if none of that existed, I'd still want you with me." His mouth curved into a charismatic smile. "Relax, you don't have to fight me. I'm not the enemy."

Lily closed her eyes against the window light and Damon, and knew there was no point arguing now. She'd have to work it out when they got back. When she wasn't so bone-tired.

But first, though she might not like the answer, she pushed the question out. "What else have you done?"

His thumb traced a circle on the pulse of her wrist.

"I've told Melissa to hire some extra help for the house. With two of us and soon a baby, there will be more housework, and I don't want you to lift a finger."

His smile morphed into one of tender arrogance that only he could pull off. "I'll look after you and the baby—" his voice lowered "—no matter what."

Easing out an exasperated sigh, she opened her eyes and fixed them on his. To anyone listening, it might sound like a dream offer—and no doubt it would be if they had a real marriage, based on mutual respect and love, a marriage that had a chance of survival. Then she'd have gratefully welcomed his offer—and everything else that went with it, including a physical relationship.

Or if he'd made the arrangements from consideration rather than his real motive: to keep her close, to keep his baby under his roof. Her body iced over at the thought of being trapped again where she didn't count as a real person. If she wasn't careful, her baby could end up with that fate in his or her own home.

"It's the only solution." He stroked her cheek with a crooked finger. "I plan to spoil you rotten. You'll never want to leave."

Her cheek tingled from the brush of his finger.

And therein lay the problem. Even frustrated at him and *knowing* they had no future, she feared he was right. If history repeated itself, she *might* never want to leave.

The man she wanted with every beat of her heart had promised to spoil her rotten. If only she didn't know better. If only he hadn't chosen the exact words her father had used with her mother before each game of cards.

"I'll win big this time, Audrey. You just wait. I'll spoil you rotten when I do."

And sometimes he did. He'd score a windfall and then blow it all on her mother and buying a stake into the next game.

He'd buy Lily presents, too, dolls, dresses, toys. And then get a babysitter while he took his wife out to celebrate.

But a week later he'd pawn her new dolls and toys, deaf to her pleas and wrenching sobs as he ripped them from her arms.

By the time she was six, Lily had learned not to become attached to presents or material things—they could disappear as quickly as they came.

The plane hit an air pocket, jolting her out of the memory.

She surveyed Damon's arrogant face—the confident smile on his sensual mouth, his ice-blue eyes with their distinctive black ring, the proud nose. Then steeled herself to ask in a dull voice, "Is that all? Are there any more surprises?"

He arched an eyebrow, pleased with her question. "I plan to keep surprising you but there's one more for now. I asked Melissa to set up interviews for a nanny. The good ones are booked in advance, so it's not too early to start looking. She should have some appointments set up for when we get back."

A scream built in her throat but she swallowed it back. "You should have checked with me first," she said through gritted teeth. This was a step too far. In fact, he'd overstepped her line in the sand by about a mile.

He might have fathered this child, but the decision

on who cared for her child when she couldn't was hers, and hers alone.

He raised her hand to his mouth and kissed her palm. "We needed a nanny and I've organized for one."

Her blood simmered up into seething ire. He still didn't get it? "I don't want a nanny. I've checked with my boss and arranged maternity leave. *I'll* raise this baby."

And after that leave was over, she'd be the one to arrange care. There was talk about setting up a crèche at the gallery, which would be perfect, but whatever happened, she would *not* be coerced into choosing one form of care over another.

He nodded. "I'm glad you feel that way. I want our baby to have the best and that's you. But the nanny will help. She can take the baby while you nap and she can prepare his meals. A spare set of hands."

Her jaw fell open. How dare he supervise her life— her life with her baby—this way? There was no way she'd put up with his kind of dictatorship. "Damon—"

"Look—" his brow creased in sincerity "—maybe I've worded this badly, but I'm trying to help."

Still holding her hand, he squeezed gently. "I'm trying, Lily. I want us to work."

Brain weary, emotionally drained and too exhausted to fight, her body begged for nothing more than eight uninterrupted hours of sleep. She pressed her eyes shut and wondered if his attempt to help was genuine. A first step on the path to being the kind of man she and her baby needed?

She opened one eye and looked over his features, resentment ebbing away. Despite all the anguish and the worry and the doubt…*could* Damon become that man? Even doing it all the wrong way, was he actually getting something right?

Perhaps a leopard could change his spots.

As they stood waiting for the rest of their luggage, Damon switched on his phone, then grimaced.

"I have to make a call." His quick smile served as an apology. "Wait here with the trolley."

He strode away to the carousel, talking into his earpiece. A few minutes later, he reappeared with her suitcase, still talking a mile to the minute. As he left for the luggage collection, his expression was the epitome of a hassled CEO needed elsewhere.

When he returned, he'd finished his call and held his own suitcase. "There's an emergency at work. I have to go in."

Her heart sank. It had started already. It seemed leopards couldn't change their spots after all. "Of course you do," she said, not hiding the weariness in her voice.

He put the suitcase down and cupped her shoulders. "I wanted to be there when you walked into our place for the first time." It was as close to an apology as Damon came. His hands drifted down her arms, rubbing slightly. "I'll make this up to you, I promise."

He shook his head as if he had no choice. In his mind, he probably didn't. But there were always choices. Some of Damon's had been made long ago and were nonnegotiable. Such as, business and money-accumulation came before personal concerns. Every single time.

He stepped closer and brought her against him. "We'll catch separate cabs, and I'll see you at home tonight."

Over his shoulder, Lily checked a clock suspended from the ceiling. Two o'clock.

He'd taken a stream of calls while they were away. But was it too much to ask that he at least accompany her to his new house? If he'd left her belongings at her place so she could go home, sleep, then organize the things she wanted moved, she wouldn't have minded. But he'd jumped the gun and moved her into his home. And now she'd be going, alone, to a house she'd never seen.

He relaxed his grip and she stepped back to see his face. But she saw in his eyes that he'd already left. "You're running out on me." She hated the accusing note in her voice, and in that moment she hated him, for putting it there.

He blew out a breath and ran long fingers through his hair. "There's been a snag in arrangements for my father's company."

Her weariness hit her full force. In the end, it always came back to BlakeCorp. She'd lost this battle before it had even begun. A little piece of her heart died. Time to face reality. Nothing, but nothing had changed. "You don't even own BlakeCorp yet."

He shrugged, not quite meeting her eyes. "I want everything in place for when I do."

Her sorrow balled into a tight knot. His words, perfectly reasonable words, explained her situation with exceptional clarity. Theirs was a marriage on paper, one in which they would keep their emotional distance. So why should his brush-off hurt so much?

But she knew why. She'd tasted his passion again and believed it contained more than a morsel of honesty, and now she couldn't shake those memories. He'd imprinted that glorious abandon with all its endless possibilities upon her mind and soul so that it was impossible to erase.

Calling on years of practice, she swallowed and nodded. "Go."

He took his keys from a pocket and extracted a solid silver one from the chain. "Melissa should be there. I'll call her from the cab and let her know the change of plans. But just in case, here's the front door key. It's yours."

Lily took the key and turned it in her palm. It was similar to his old house key, the one she'd posted back after they'd broken up. The first time she'd realized she couldn't rely on him. Tears rose to sting the back of her nose.

Damon brushed a tender kiss across her lips. "Come on. The sooner we get going, the sooner I can get home to you."

Five minutes later, Lily sat alone in the backseat of a cab, the familiar feeling of abandonment growing stronger until it almost suffocated her.

The thing was, against her better judgment, she'd actually started to believe he could be there for her. That arranging for help—though not what she wanted or expected—was a step in the right direction.

But yet again he'd prioritized his work over her needs. Moving her into his house then letting her find it on her own showed her that, as clearly as if he'd handed her a note outlining his intentions.

She released a bitter laugh. Why should she be surprised? Based on past experience, she should have expected more of the same. For him, money came before people, even his wife and child. And *that* was why she had no future with Damon Blakely.

Six

Damon woke the next morning in his spare bedroom, curled around Lily. He smiled sleepily. What an excellent way to start the day.

He leaned in an inch, pulled her silky blond hair to the side and placed a delicate kiss to the back of her neck.

She stirred and rolled to face him, eyes opening slowly. The pleasure he saw deep in her forest-green eyes sent a bolt of satisfaction through his system...until wariness replaced her happiness.

With a primal need to banish the interloping caution, he kissed her lips, gently, teasing, the way he knew she liked. He'd rouse more pleasure in her body than she could stand...and, damn it, he'd restore that special joy to her eyes. An irresistible impulse, deep inside, demanded it.

He pulled her closer, inserting a knee between hers,

not breaking the kiss, then pulled her closer again, so his thigh pressed into the juncture of her legs.

He knew she wasn't one hundred percent happy with her decision to stay but he had more than one means of making himself indispensable. He'd give her all she could ever want with his money—materially and with staff—and all she could dream of with his body.

She was his. She and their baby.

And suddenly he knew this wasn't just about BlakeCorp anymore—not that it had ever been the whole picture.

Something more fundamental was involved, a compelling force coming from his solar plexus.

He cupped her face, channeling all his emotion into the kiss. A delicate moan of desire came from deep within her as their roles shifted and she tugged at him, reaching to his hips and finding him naked. A purr of satisfaction greeted the discovery and in return he slid her satin nightgown over her head.

He'd never get tired of feeling her skin on his. And now they were married, he never had to. For the rest of his life, he'd spend his nights making love to her and wake with her each morning. He'd drive all her doubts away.

Growling with the thrill of conquest, he rolled onto his back, taking her with him to sprawl across his ready body. Her eyes flashed with unadulterated lust and she pulled away, straightening, straddling him, raising herself into position, then lowering to bring him into heaven on earth.

His hands shot out of their own volition and gripped

her hips, planting her there, holding her firm as he bucked and buried himself as deep as possible.

Her movements slowed to a stop. She flattened her lips as that damned wariness returned, claiming her features.

She closed her eyes. "I promised myself we wouldn't do this again," she whispered.

Damon sucked in a deep breath through his teeth and held his protesting body in check while he processed her words. "We're married. It's not a sin, Lily," he rasped.

A pained expression crossed her face. "But it's not right, either."

He took a patient breath. He should have expected this reluctance. Just like on their wedding night, she clung to her doubts because theirs wasn't the traditional hearts-and-flowers courtship. But she was very wrong. They belonged together.

And now he needed a strategy before her resistance went too far. He searched her gaze, and one thing became crystal clear. She might have said she didn't want this, but she didn't want to stop any more than he did—despite her words, she hadn't moved a muscle to leave.

He reached to stroke her shoulder and along her arm. "It feels right to me, sweetheart. And maybe that's all that matters here and now." He ran his hand down her side and she shivered. "You. Me. Feeling right together."

She moved against him once and bit down on her lip. "What about afterward?"

He cupped her face. "We'll handle afterward when it happens."

He pulled her down and kissed her slowly, sensuously. "Come. Live in the moment with me." He coaxed her velvet lips, determined to make her see they belonged together.

She moaned her assent then rose up above him once more.

His hands slid up, touching her everywhere at once, lingering over her breasts and their puckered tips, moving down to slip between the place where they joined to take her higher.

She moved against him again.

"Yes," he groaned.

His eyes swept over her, silver-blond hair spilled across her shoulders, alabaster skin glowing with her desire, riding him like an erotic Lady Godiva.

How had he survived the months without her in his bed?

He gently grasped her shoulders and pulled her down, kissed her mouth hard, held her against him, as close as possible now he felt ready to explode, listened to her release echo in his ears and let it tip him over the edge, to the place where only he and Lily existed.

Boneless, he lay across his sheets with Lily's sweat-slicked body draped over him. Nirvana could hold no more pleasure than this.

Relishing the sensation, he lay still for long minutes. Then, floating down from cloud nine, his thoughts turned to the future. Their future. Their baby.

"Have you had any ideas about names for the baby?" he murmured.

A dreamy smile transformed her face as she slid to his side and stretched. She bent her elbow and propped her head in her palm. "I've got a mental list, but nothing I'm sure of. Have you given it any thought?"

A lot of thought actually, including on the drive home from work the night before. "If it's a girl, what about naming her after your gran? Pearl."

Her mouth rounded in surprise, then softened. "That's what you want? After Gran?"

He ran a finger down her cheek. "I'll be forever indebted to her—she saved the mother of my child. Expecting my own son or daughter has made me think about how she protected you."

Her eyes misted over but she smiled. "I've been thinking of that, too. And it's a gorgeous name. Pearl Blakely."

Giving thanks for this harmony, so rare between them lately, he placed a delicate kiss on her shoulder. "What about a middle name?"

Her hand fluttered to the silver heart pendant hanging from her neck. "I've been thinking Theresa would be perfect."

Damon stilled. She wanted to give his mother's name to their child? An unexpected lump formed in his throat. "I'd like that. Pearl Theresa Blakely."

Lily's hands smoothed across her naked stomach as she whispered, "What do you think, Pearl?"

Damon chuckled. "What if junior's a boy?"

Her smile grew. "I'd like Michael, for your father. I wish I'd met him."

His throat thickened again, and he cleared it before replying. "He would have loved you. Both my parents would have."

"Thank you." She swallowed then met his gaze. "I chose the first name for a boy. Do you want to choose the middle name?"

He thought for a moment. He'd considered many options last night, but only one felt right. "Andrew. Michael Blakely is from my side of the family tree, so I think Andrew from your middle name, Andrea."

Tears filled her eyes as he drew her close again. "Michael Andrew Blakely or Pearl Theresa Blakely," she said. "I like them."

He nuzzled into the curve of her neck. "And the room next door to the main bedroom—our room—would make a good nursery for Pearl or Michael. We'll be on hand during the night."

She took a moment to respond. "Pardon?"

He'd already worked out some of the details as he'd drifted off to sleep last night. It made complete sense. "I'll move the home office equipment to the room down the hall. We can knock a connecting door through—" he looked around the spare room, assessing its walls in proxy "—maybe add—"

Lily slid away and gathered the sheet around her torso. "Damon, if I've misled you, I didn't mean to. Just because we're sharing a moment here doesn't mean things have changed. Maybe I haven't made myself clear enough. Separate rooms. Separate lives." She paused with raised brows. "Pearl or Michael will have a nursery beside *my* room."

He frowned. No, she hadn't been clear at all. He'd told her on the plane he was trying to make their marriage work and she'd seemed happy. He'd thought she was giving them another chance. Granted, she'd slept in a spare room, not in his suite where all her things were, but he couldn't always follow the workings of the female mind. He'd assumed it had something to do with him not being there.

And she'd been a little reluctant making love just now, though nothing she didn't want to be talked through.

He held back a sigh and turned on a charming smile instead. He wasn't worried. He always won—sometimes the end result took a bit more work than others. But he wouldn't begrudge the effort when the windfall was as important as Lily and his child.

He took her hand and rubbed a thumb across her palm. "Lily, I meant what I said before. This feels right."

She shook her head. "There's too much at stake for me to be that simplistic. Damon, I won't compromise my baby's emotional well-being. I've told you I will not raise my child in a family where money is all-important and nothing and no one is more a priority than Daddy's work. I'll move out and raise this baby on my own before I let that happen."

His shoulders bunched and his grip tightened on her hand. "I'll make our baby a priority." He meant it down to the soles of his feet. "Securing our child's financial future is part of that. Making sure he has his grandfather's company to inherit when he's old enough *is* making our baby a priority."

He bit back the beginnings of impatience at her insistence that he wouldn't be a good father. He knew what was best for them all—being a family unit. Why was that so hard for her to see?

Lily's mouth opened and closed as if searching for words before she said, "This isn't about money. Do you know the drug addiction and suicide rates among rich kids?" She shook her head, as if world-weary. "Money doesn't buy happiness. I'm talking about love and *time* with her or him."

A memory flashed before his eyes of growing up with neither of those things, and he inwardly flinched. But he was nothing like his uncle. No question, his child's upbringing would be poles apart from his own. "I can do that, too." He leaned over and kissed the tip of her nose. "Just promise me you'll consider the nursery."

One step at a time. That's how the best deals were secured.

Lily rolled her eyes, but not before a flash of resignation surfaced. "You're not used to the word *no,* are you?"

"Actually, I am," he said with a straight face. "As a child I heard it far too many times from my aunt and uncle and I developed an allergy to it. Now I avoid it as much as possible."

The tension from thinking about his childhood eased from his shoulders before a grin tugged one corner of his mouth, softening the sentiment further. He could phrase it lightly to her but he was deadly serious. He hated being told no, and intended to hear yes from Lily's mouth sometime very soon.

She looked as if she didn't know whether to laugh or strangle him. Instead she flung back the covers and headed for the bathroom. "I have to go back to work today. We'll continue this later."

Damon laced his hands behind his head on the pillow and smiled.

A little extra work, a dose of humor, and he'd won this battle. Likewise he'd also win the war.

Lily looked around Damon's kitchen—she still couldn't call it *their* kitchen—bathed in mid-Sunday morning light…then she glanced at the ceiling.

Directly above her was the room Damon had earmarked as a nursery. She'd said she wanted the nursery beside her room, yet she'd been spending her nights in Damon's….

She shook her head and focused instead on the baking aromas that filled her senses and calmed her. Not that they'd be able to eat the entire tray of blueberry muffins, apple pie, sultana cookies, banana bread *and* fairy cakes, but she felt better having made them all. She could drop some off to Gran in the afternoon and freeze the rest.

She'd learned to cook from Gran, but had never wanted to bake this much before. Probably a nesting instinct—which made sense considering she'd repressed all other forms of that particular urge.

A nursery would have been an obvious place to channel her maternal yearnings, but she hadn't set foot in the room above the kitchen even once. It'd haunted her, though, on the fringes of her awareness where she had no control.

She glanced again at the ceiling, then felt herself turn toward the stairs, ignoring her well-developed sense of self-preservation. She climbed the stairs quickly, pausing at the top, then padded down the hall to the room next to Damon's.

They'd been home—married—for nine days and she'd immersed herself in her work at the gallery most of that time, but this weekend, her thoughts were almost exclusively on the baby and their lives together.

Slowly, almost reverently, she opened the door and slipped inside, barely daring to breathe. After that first night back in Melbourne she'd begun to temporarily share Damon's expansive room. Partly because she'd been too exhausted to move her things into the spare room, and partly because a tiny tendril of hope refused to be squashed.

Ridiculous. She *knew* they had no future—she'd made that decision already. Yet, when she was still or quiet, her heart whispered, *What if this could work? If there's a chance, isn't it worth the risk?*

She shook her head and laid her hands over her belly, feeling the comfort of the cotton and the small, hard mound beneath. Excitement for the precious child growing within her womb flared.

God, she wished it *could* work. Perhaps if she gave it a month or two, saw how it panned out…

Lily snorted a laugh. She was her mother's daughter, clutching at straws. She ran a fingertip along the windowpane and surveyed Damon's paved courtyard.

Peculiar how they'd fallen into somewhat of a routine, sharing a bed at night, acting as if theirs was a normal marriage as they left for their jobs during the day. She'd attended her checkup and been given the all clear. Melissa left dinner in the oven for them each night, even though Lily had told her she didn't need to.

Damon sometimes worked late and on weekends—

like today. So she'd eaten alone five of the eight nights, as she had when they were dating. She'd begun bringing work home for her next exhibition, on surrealists. It gave her something to do other than dwell on thoughts of this room.

The wisp of hope that her heart nurtured had inspired dreams of transforming the room into a child's wonderland, close to both mummy and daddy, and she couldn't bear to crush it completely.

She walked to the far corner, visualizing a crib draped in the finest cream lace, the place her baby would lay its head. She glanced left and imagined a chest of drawers topped with fluffy animals. If she reached out, she could almost touch them....

Downstairs, she heard a key in the lock and her heart leaped as if she were a child caught with her hand in the cookie jar. She couldn't risk encouraging Damon's confidence in his plans for the nursery, *his* plans for their future.

She slipped out of the room, securing the door behind her, then rushed down the stairs, pulse racing. As Damon's footsteps echoed across the tiled floor, she stepped into the kitchen, trying to bring her breathing back under control.

"My mouth started watering as soon as I stepped out of the car." Strong arms wrapped around her from behind and she smiled, heart still racing, as she melted back into her husband's warmth and strength. Moments like these, where she could pretend the past and future didn't exist, were glorious slivers of time where everything was perfect.

Making love in Damon's bed allowed her that same miracle, where she could block out reality and let her fragile hope take wings. Live completely in the moment.

He nuzzled the sensitive spot behind her ear and her blood heated. "I could smell your muffins from the garage, Mrs. Blakely. I swear, your baking even beats Melissa's."

Lily turned in his arms, threading her hands under his suit jacket, and kissed him. "I've just boiled the jug if you'd like a coffee and a slice of apple pie."

"I've got a better idea for my mouth." He leaned in and met her lips in a slow promise that heated her insides.

Then he pulled back, eyes roaming her face. "You're flushed. Is it from the cooking or did you rush to greet me?" His fingers brushed her cheeks. "Tell me you were upstairs starting on the nursery," he said against her lips.

Her mouth tugged to one side to disguise her grin. He just wouldn't give in. "Asking me the same question every day won't increase the chances of getting the answer you want."

He rested his forehead on hers. "It can't hurt."

His persistence gave her fledgling hope another surge of life. Maybe they could make this work....

She took a deep breath, held it, then released it in a rush. "I've decided to give us two months to see how things work out."

A grin spread across his face. He probably believed his charm had worked its magic again. Perhaps it had.

Her pragmatic side kicked herself for giving in, for being gullible enough to *believe,* but in that moment, her optimism and hope won out.

She laid her palms flat on his chest. "If, at the end of the two months, I think we have a future, then we'll discuss the nursery being beside your room. But, Damon, you need to be committed, as well."

"Sweetheart, you have no idea how committed I am to this." He captured her mouth and she lost all sense of time and place.

An eternity—or was it merely minutes?—later, he pulled back and cupped her face in his hands, his face solemn. "I'll make you happy, I swear. In fact, I want to add another vow to the ones we took in Auckland." His voice deepened. "I vow that I, Damon, will keep you, Lily, in a state of perfect happiness at every opportunity."

He kissed her lips slowly, reverentially. "I'll make *sure* this marriage works."

There was something magical in the moment, almost more meaningful than when they'd exchanged wedding vows. Almost too intense. She raised her hand to smooth the hair from his forehead. "Damon, you can't make it happen through the force of your will—"

He placed a finger over her lips. "Our wedding may have been rushed but I want this to last our lifetime. Beyond that. And I know you're not sure yet, but I'll keep working hard until you are." He kissed her top lip, then the bottom one. "I promise you."

The shrill ring of the phone on the kitchen counter snapped her back to reality. Damon reached behind him and picked up the receiver, keeping one arm firmly around her.

He answered then passed it to her, curiosity in his frown. "It's for you."

Her heart skipped a beat as she took the phone. The only person who had Damon's number was her grandmother. She'd told everyone else to reach her on her cell phone. Her stomach knotted. Even though Gran was on the road to recovery and had moved into the new house Damon had bought her with the on-site nurse, Lily couldn't help but worry.

"Hello? Gran?" Lily stepped back to lean on the counter behind her, watching Damon sample the banana bread.

"Lily Blakely?" the thin voice of an unfamiliar man asked.

One of Gran's doctors? Her lungs constricted. She clasped the phone tighter. "Yes."

"I'm Ian Crawford, one of the attorneys acting for Travis Blakely."

Relief for Gran quickly transformed into a lead weight in her stomach, one that was completely unrelated to her pregnancy. Why hadn't the attorney spoken to Damon?

"Mr. Blakely has requested that you visit him—alone, this morning—on a matter of utmost urgency." The thin voice raised a notch as if underlining his words.

Lily gripped the counter with her free hand. She hated being near Travis Blakely. He was both cruel and intimidating—an abhorrent combination. But the hairs standing up on the back of her neck whispered, as much as she might not want to, perhaps she should hear this man out. "He wants me to come alone?"

Damon's head snapped around, eyes locked on hers. He'd seen her fear. She shifted her gaze and focused on the fruit bowl on the opposite counter.

"Yes. As soon as you can get here. I can't stress the

urgency enough." The man paused then said in a rush, "Within the hour would be preferable." He disconnected with an audible click.

Lily stared ahead, unseeing, mind rushing from one implausible scenario to the next. Was this a trick? She reached past Damon to hang up the phone but he took the receiver from her, replacing it himself.

"You've gone pale." He moved closer, taking her hands and rubbing them between his own, as if trying to bring the warmth back to her cold extremities. "What did he say?" he demanded, his concern iced with anger.

She struggled to arrange her jumble of thoughts into a coherent reply. "Your uncle wants to see me this morning. Alone."

Damon's face hardened to stone. "Like hell."

Lily bit down on her lip. "His lawyer said it was urgent."

"I don't care what his lawyer says." His eyes narrowed in determination.

"It's obviously something to do with the will." Her baby's inheritance, and the lynchpin in the deal with Damon to look after Gran for the rest of her life. "He can't have anything to say to either one of us about anything else." Surely it wouldn't take long. She could face another ten minutes of that man's revolting company when the outcome meant so much to those she loved.

Damon's jaw clenched. "All the more reason why you shouldn't see him alone. I'll go instead."

A bud of resistance to Damon's high-handed manner reared its head, even as she recognized his response as concern. If their relationship had any future at all, she must keep a spine of steel and not let him dictate every choice they made. This will involved her as much as him. "What if his attorney has a question for me?"

He shrugged. "I can answer for you."

Something inside her snapped. She was tired of having decisions made for her. Her back straightened. "He asked to see me. Alone. I'm going. Alone."

Heat and approval flared in his eyes. "I was right. You'll be the perfect mother for our child. You'll be a protective momma bear." He smiled, seemingly satisfied. "We'll go together."

It was probably the biggest concession she'd wrest from him. She'd seen his determined glint before. She blew out a breath and nodded. Better she conserved her energy for facing Travis Blakely.

Lily watched Damon from the corner of her eye as he drove the distance to his childhood home. He'd been silent since he'd started the Lexus, his hands clenched tight on the steering wheel and his shoulders tense.

Finally she faced him. "You've told him about the wedding and the baby?"

Damon spared her a curt nod as he pulled off the road into Travis Blakely's large circular driveway.

She turned back and watched the mansion come into view. Stark white and two stories high, the front was the length of eight rooms, all with floor-to-ceiling windows, permanently shuttered. The only word that suited the structure was *imposing*. She supposed that was why Travis liked it.

This place would come to her baby one day. Tears stung her eyes. Although her child inheriting a home with an unhappy legacy chilled her, she knew legacies could be changed. Relief surged. Their child would never be homeless. He or she would have a rock-solid asset. This home couldn't be ripped away. Their child belonged here, and she was prepared to fight for that.

She thought of Travis and shuddered. If only it hadn't been such a soulless building.

Everything about the Blakely mansion was unbearably cold. But once Travis was gone, perhaps this house could become the loving safe haven she'd wanted for her child. Or maybe, with everything that had happened here, that was too much to ask of the bricks and mortar before her. How had Damon survived his childhood here—with Travis?

Lost in thought, she didn't notice Damon had left his seat until he opened her door. Accepting his hand, she stepped out. Even in the midst of the cocktail of fear and determination, Damon's touch still brought tingles to her fingers and simmering heat to her blood.

He gave her fingers a squeeze. "I'm right here." Despite his supportive tone, she felt the tension radiating from his body.

She smiled back and let him lead her to the front door. They were met by a short, lean man with a comb-over of long gray hairs.

"Mrs. Blakely?" His thin voice was familiar from his earlier call.

Lily nodded. Damon thrust his hand toward the man. "And Mr. Blakely."

The man sighed. "He said you'd come with her. I'm Ian Crawford. Come in."

They walked across the black marble floor through the foyer and into the vast receiving room where the party had been held less than three weeks earlier. The room, although light and airy from the two-story ceiling and masses of glass, maintained the cold, stark atmosphere of the dark foyer.

Damon's reassuring hand on her waist kept her from bolting, or losing the banana bread she'd had for breakfast. "Do you know what this is about, Crawford?"

The other man stopped and turned back. "He's ailing."

Damon's face remained impassive. "He was ailing two and a half weeks ago when I saw him."

Crawford shook his head, concern pinching his features. "He's worse. Much worse. His heart is the least of his worries now—his liver and kidneys are failing. The doctors have given him only days."

Lily's skin broke out in goose bumps. If she could ever hate a person, it'd be this old man for what he'd done to Damon. But she couldn't bear to think of anyone in pain or fear. Travis Blakely must be in both. Her newfound sympathy warred with her abhorrence for the bully, which still gripped her insides, leaving her stomach clenched and churning.

Days to live… She'd been so sure, but was this meeting truly about the will, or something less straightforward?

Crawford turned to her and shifted his weight from foot to foot. "He wanted to see you, Mrs. Blakely, most urgently." His eyes flicked to Damon, then back. "And he was insistent that it be alone."

Damon pulled her in closer. "Not going to happen."

She'd never had anyone besides Gran willing to

stand by her. Until now. The thought soothed some of her disquiet. She looked up at her husband with a softened gaze. "He's in no position to intimidate me. I'll see him alone."

Damon kept his eyes on Crawford. "No."

Crawford nervously cleared his throat. "The nurse refuses to let more than one person in his room at a time."

Damon merely grunted.

A sinking feeling enveloped her as she pictured Travis looking from her to Damon and being reluctant to talk because she'd defied him and brought his nephew. If something went awry with his will and Travis decided to leave everything to his cousin's son, Mark, what would happen to her deal with Damon to look after Gran and their baby?

She was prepared to face the devil himself if it meant protecting her child and Gran.

If Crawford were to be believed, time was running out to hear what Travis wanted to say. To ensure the will remained as it stood.

"Damon—" she swallowed, her throat suddenly too tight "—I need to see him alone."

Damon looked down at her, his ice-blue eyes calculating. "And I need to hear anything he has to say to you."

She felt the power of his demand and was acutely aware of being trapped between two powerful men. A precarious position.

But she was no longer the naive girl Damon had dated all those months ago. Coping with her relationship breakdown with Damon, and now her impending motherhood had changed her. It was up to her to ensure her family was safe. She simply had to face the lion's den.

She laid her hand over Damon's as it held her waist. "I need to do this. And Crawford said the nurse won't let us in together. I'm a grown woman, Damon. I can go alone."

A myriad of emotions crossed Damon's face before he blew out a breath and nodded once. "I'm coming with you as far as the door, though. And you'll tell me word for word what the old bastard says."

Lily smiled up at him. "I promise."

They walked the stairs behind Crawford in silence and with each step, the tension in her stomach coiled tighter. A continuous loop of questions and self-doubt ran through her mind: should they challenge the nurse to let Damon see Travis with her? How would Travis look this close to death? Was he really dying, or was it a bluff?

And always, the awareness of Damon's firm hand on her waist escorting her, his solid male warmth and strength steadying her. As much as was possible for what now felt like a trip to the gallows.

On the third step from the top she stumbled but Damon deftly caught her before she lost balance.

Outside his uncle's bedroom, Damon brushed a kiss across her forehead and released her. A muscle ticked in his jaw as he clenched and unclenched, clenched and unclenched. "Don't believe anything that tyrant says," he ground out.

Her insides went cold before she dismissed the feeling and nodded. Then she summoned all her courage, opened the door and walked through.

A grave, red-haired nurse stood beside the bed, monitoring several machines that would have looked more at home in a hospital ward. Travis lay beneath covers, looking smaller than she remembered. Lily bit down on her lip and managed to suppress a gasp. An oxygen tube ran under his nose and several other tubes came out from under the blankets. But his eyes were as sharp as ever.

She took a step closer and the nurse looked up with an unwelcoming frown. "You must be Mrs. Blakely. Are you sure your business here is a priority?"

Lily hesitated, fingers gripping the door handle behind her. "I have no idea what my business here is, or its importance. I was summoned."

The nurse passed a judgmental gaze over Lily, then across to Travis. "I think I'll stay."

The old man coughed and spluttered then, despite his obvious frailty, fixed the nurse with a commanding stare. "Go," he wheezed.

Clearly reluctant, the nurse studied Lily a moment longer before shaking her head and pointing to a button attached to the bed head. "Buzz at the first sign of a problem."

Lily nodded, still processing the scene before her, stomach in knots, as the nurse marched out the door.

"Come closer, girl," Travis rasped.

Tears of pity welled in her eyes, but she held them back, one of Gran's favorite sayings playing in her mind. *What goes around comes around.* He was a bitter old vulture who didn't deserve her sympathy. She waited for him to speak.

The wait was short.

"I have things to say…and little energy." He paused, taking several shallow breaths. "Excuse me…if I come straight…to the point."

Lily sat in the high-backed chair beside the bed in what was obviously the nurse's usual position. "Of course."

"I hear…you married him." Hate-filled eyes burned in his ashen face.

A strong urge to defend Damon from the man who'd tormented him through childhood destroyed the little sympathy she'd felt. But she folded her hands together on her lap, determined to at least hear the old man out. "I did."

"Told you why?" he wheezed.

She nodded. "He told me about the will."

He looked frustrated for a moment, as if she'd destroyed his fun in revealing that information. Then his eyes regained their sly glint.

"Know what game…he's playing?"

About to reply, she hesitated. "What do you mean?"

"I mean—" he struggled for breath "—what he's after."

"Damon wants BlakeCorp back. And I don't blame him." BlakeCorp should always have been his; of course he'd try to get it back.

"BlakeCorp…is a front—" he closed his eyes, resting them, then dragged them open again "—for his real…agenda."

The little spark of hope that had been growing during the days at Damon's house flickered, seeming more vulnerable that it'd been before.

"Your husband…wants only revenge…against me." He gasped for air, struggling as if it were a near impossible task. "Destroy me. Everything else…even you…is expendable…to his…obsession."

Her awareness shrank to just the cunning, frail man in front of her and his meaning. Expendable? To an obsession with destroying his uncle? He was only after BlakeCorp....

The thought died as she remembered a snatch of phone conversation she'd overheard when Damon had been speaking to his assistant, Macy. *"Consequences be damned. Ignore Travis's lawyers. I want that company."*

She'd thought he was talking about BlakeCorp— but, now she thought about it, why would he need to make arrangements when it would come to him via the will? The rosy picture she'd been painting of Damon began to flicker and blur.

She met Travis's reptilian eyes. "He bought one of your companies."

"Two."

She gripped the sides of her chair and brought the rosy picture back into focus. Travis was scheming again. Damon bought and sold companies every day. It could easily happen that two of them had belonged to Travis.

She would not believe the man she loved was capable of the brutality of destroying someone.

Seven

A blow of surprise slammed into her chest as she realized how her mind had phrased the thought.

She loved him.

Oh, dear God, *she loved him*.

Still gripping the sides of the chair, she dug her fingers in until the pressure turned to pain.

She'd never stopped loving Damon. And if she could love him even through this mess, she'd probably never stop.

Closing her eyes, she bit back a groan. Of course she loved him. She never would have gone along with this marriage, the lovemaking, him moving her into his house if she hadn't. She'd just been too afraid of the consequences to face the fact.

But what of *his* heart? Had all the kind words and

sweet lovemaking merely been a facade? A mask covering his true nature?

No, she *wouldn't* believe it.

Her eyes fluttered open and fixed on the ornate headboard. She wasn't naive, she knew Damon was capable of morally questionable behavior, it was why she hadn't wanted to get involved with him again. But these last few days had been *real*. He cared for her and their baby. He wasn't the monster Travis was implying.

Clenching her hands tightly on her lap, she narrowed her eyes at Travis.

"Have made…arrangements." Travis turned his head to a folder on a small table beside her.

She looked at the plain manila folder with her heart in her mouth. It would be filled with poison, no doubt about it. She didn't want to touch it, to be dragged further under the sea of chaos and confusion that already buffeted her.

Again Travis turned his head toward the folder, his pale, gnarled face burning with intent. "Important."

She hated this man, could never forgive his treatment of Damon as a child, but she'd come here to hear him out. Because he held all the cards with regard to the inheritance. She had no choice other than to do as Travis bid her.

She reached toward the folder and opened it.

Last Will and Testament of Travis Nicholas Blakely.

She bit down on her lip. Reading its contents did not mean she'd let herself be hijacked by the old man's schemes.

Travis wheezed twice, trying to speak before he gained enough control to form words. "Made changes… when knew…about baby."

Thoughts in such turmoil that her fingers felt clumsy, Lily skimmed through the first page. It was short and to the point. And then her turmoil ceased as her body went numb.

"Everything goes to me," she whispered.

Travis nodded.

She kept reading, barely believing. "You're leaving me *everything?*"

Again, Travis nodded. "For…baby. So he'll…always have…everything…he needs."

She turned the page, frowning, and slowly comprehending. He was leaving her a multimillion-dollar empire of business holdings and personal assets.

Her mind clicked into gear. *No matter what happened, her child would always be secure.* And she could look after Gran herself.

Yet, along with the relief, it felt odd to know this slip of paper afforded her the stability and financial security that had been denied her in earlier life. A heavy weight that felt as if it'd always been sitting on her shoulders fell and smashed into a thousand pieces, bringing glorious relief trickling through her veins.

But, dear God, what would Damon say?

"Money in…envelope."

Numbness beginning to lift now, Lily picked up the envelope and found a wad of cash inside.

Why had he done this? He was spiteful enough to have instigated this purely out of hatred for his nephew. And when Damon found out, he'd be outraged. She'd share everything with him, of course, but she couldn't bear to think of his reaction, or her own until her jumble of thoughts settled down into some kind of logical order.

Holding the cash in one hand and the copy of the will in the other, she looked to Travis for explanation.

"Tide…you over. Legalities…take time. Two hundred…thousand."

Lily had never held that much money in her hands. A buzz started in her ears. She had to ask. "What about Damon?"

"You don't…need him…anymore." But Travis wasn't smirking in victory, he looked strangely—earnest. "Raise baby…away. Don't let him…be…like us."

His eyes drifted closed and Lily wondered if he'd fallen asleep before he opened them again—a new, raw emotion now there. "Take…care…of…baby. Tell…him—" he broke off, eyes shining with unshed tears "—about…me."

Everything stilled—the room, her heart, even Travis—as she saw the old man show something resembling love for the first time since she'd known him. Even while a part of her wondered how this tyrant could feel this way over the seed of his despised nephew, to another part of her it made sense. Something more lay behind the man she'd thought of as rhino-tough. A small, well-hidden shred of humanity.

The door creaked open and the red-haired nurse appeared, frowning. "If he's been talking to you since I've been gone, he'll need to rest. He doesn't have much stamina."

Lily forced a smile, relieved to be set free from this room of emotional land mines, yet not wanting to leave until she had her feelings in a manageable state. Or at least till she knew *what* she felt. She put the money back in the envelope and picked up the copy of the will.

Could she accept so much money? Though, it wasn't for her—he'd done it for the baby. A baby Travis had every right to provide for. In fact, this was the same plan she'd agreed to with Damon, with one small change. Everything was in her name.

She held all the cards.

The experience was as unfamiliar as it was overwhelming. No matter what happened from here on, two things were now ensured. Her precious baby would always be safe and secure. And Gran would live out her days in as much luxury as she would accept. She could stop worrying about the future, and just live. Her face relaxed and tears stung the backs of her eyes.

This was a different financial security to being Damon's wife. Yes, that would ensure she had money, but it would have been *his* money. It could be taken again or disappear in an instant the way her father's money had repeatedly done. But this new will meant the money would be hers and the baby's, and she'd make sure that not one cent was squandered. She'd give her baby the financial stability she'd been denied.

But now Travis had done this, would Damon fight it in court?

She hesitated beside the bed, catching the old man's eye. The words *thank you* trembled on her lips but she couldn't bring herself to say them. Instinctively she knew there was more to this gift than appeared on the surface. Travis knew exactly what he'd done in raising questions in her mind, hoping to drive a wedge into her marriage.

It was time to leave, to tell Damon what had happened. Yet, she was loath to face him, his questions, the answers she needed to give and the decisions she would need to make.

And to ask the question she dreaded most of all.

Damon paced again down the corridor outside his uncle's room, his gut twisting in knots. His own childhood bedroom was at the end of the hall but he had no desire to revisit it—there were no loving memories stored there. Just the ghost of a boy huddled in the corner, crying for his parents and shaking in fear of his uncle.

Banishing the vision, he clenched his fists and turned to face the door that hid Lily. The nurse had returned a good five minutes ago. Where was Lily? What was that evil man saying to her? He'd been searching his brain to come up with probabilities, as well as contingency plans to minimize their effects. He already had his second-in-charge, Macy, on standby, ready for damage control with his business holdings.

He stared at the door, willing it to open. Lily might not realize it but that man in there was an incarnation of the devil. The man who'd taken everything from him twice. He could almost feel the ulcer form as his stomach burned.

The door creaked open and Lily slipped out, a large envelope and papers in her hand, her face as pale as fine bone china. God, what had he said to her?

Two strides and he was by her side. "Tell me what he said."

Her forest-green eyes searched his face, looking for something. "Not here," she whispered.

She was right. The old man probably had spies waiting to eavesdrop. He put a supportive arm around her and led her downstairs and out to the car. "Home?"

An emotion he couldn't identify flashed across her face but was gone within moments. "Yes."

He ushered her out and into the car, flexing his hands on the steering wheel as he drove out the driveway.

He'd fully intended waiting until they reached home before asking, but the questions gnawed at his gut. "Tell me."

She moistened her lips and took a deep breath. "He talked about our marriage. About you. He said..." She frowned and folded her arms before picking up the sentence again. "He said you didn't want just Blake-Corp. More than anything else in your life—more than me—you wanted to destroy him."

The knot of red-hot hate for his uncle exploded to life, becoming the familiar seething monster. He accelerated fast to overtake a truck. Damn that old bastard! On his deathbed and still trying to stir up trouble. Was his anger at his older brother so strong that he had to torment his nephew even with his last breath?

"Damon?" Her voice wobbled. "*Are* you obsessed with destroying him?"

"Of course I want to see him annihilated more than anything." As soon as the words were out of his mouth he desperately wanted them back, knowing she'd take them the wrong way. His gut clenched. "But there are other things I want, too," he said, backpedaling. "You, for example. Our baby."

He glanced over and saw horror in her every feature.

"Oh, come on, Lily. Don't believe the venom of a bitter old man." He reached for her hand but she drew it back, pushing herself against the door, putting as much space between them as she could.

"I didn't believe him. Not completely." Her voice wavered, then found strength—and anger. "But I do believe *you*. What I just heard you say. You mentioned wanting me as an *example*. Your wife and baby. You're too full of hatred and anger to ever see us as anything more. And I…I really thought we had a chance this time…" She trailed off, as if she couldn't bear to say any more.

He slowed for a red light, perspiration breaking out over his forehead. His chance for a future with Lily was disappearing before his eyes. No, no, this could be salvaged. "Lily, it just came out the wrong way. You know how I feel about you—about the baby."

"You know what, Damon? I *do* know how you feel about us. You desire me. You're interested in the baby, probably more than you thought you would be. But you look at us and you see one thing—access to your uncle's fortune. Everything comes back to your uncle. It's never just about us."

The traffic light changed and he accelerated, heart thumping, mind racing, trying to find a way out. The only answer he came up with was making her face reality.

He dragged in a breath. "Lily, we both went into this marriage with our eyes open. This was never a love match. You're right, I desire you. Even now when we're fighting. And you're right that I'm interested in our baby—more than that, I *want* this baby."

He ran a hand through his hair, blood pounding in

his head. He needed to get these words perfect. "You're also right that I want access to his worldly goods. Not for the money, you know that. For my father's company. It was supposed to be mine." His father had left it to his younger brother, Travis, along with all of his assets, on the understanding that he'd pass what was left, after the cost of raising his nephew, to Damon when he came of age.

But his father had been too trusting. Not a mistake Damon would make.

He swung into his garage, cut the engine and turned to her. "And if I can find other ways to hurt a man who has made it his life's ambition to humiliate me and deprive me of what's mine, then I'm not sorry about that."

She looked away from him, out the window, and spoke softly. "You don't feel anything more strongly than your hate. Our marriage—*I* can never compete. We have nothing."

Something in his chest clenched and coiled. How could she think that after everything they'd shared? He reached for her hand and interlaced their fingers. "No, Lily. We have the two of us, living as husband and wife, desiring each other, expecting our first child. That's enough for me, more than I thought I'd ever get." He laid their joined hands on her thigh, caressing the tension she was carrying in all of her body. Then she relaxed and he breathed a sigh of relief.

She turned to him, her eyes swimming with unshed tears. "Travis changed his will."

Damon felt his blood pressure skyrocket as the seething monster thrashed against his ribs, threatening to take full control, to demand answers. Yet he kept his voice evenly modulated. "Tell me."

She withdrew her hand and fidgeted with the envelope and papers in her lap. "He's leaving everything to me."

His mind sprang into action, subduing the monster, creating scenarios, calculating possibilities. He couldn't tell Lily that Travis didn't own the assets in the will to pass them on. Not even Travis or his solicitors knew. Travis's preference for secret dealings had kept him and his legal team in the dark perfectly about this bombshell.

As of this morning, Damon owned the lot. Even BlakeCorp. Everything.

He had to keep that part secret, because if Lily couldn't understand his need for retribution, she'd *never* understand this. She'd always abhorred secrets of any kind and this was the mother of them all. Perhaps if he'd told her from the start…

But now he would cover his tracks and she'd never know there had been any deception.

"He also gave me a sum of cash to tide me over until his estate is settled." She raised her chin almost imperceptibly. "I'll share everything he bequeaths me with you. In fact, I probably have to as your spouse, which is fine with me. But I'm leaving, Damon. What we had might be more than enough for you, but I can't be in a relationship with someone who's obsessed with hate and destruction."

Before he could process the words, she'd stepped out of the car and marched inside.

An hour later, Lily heard the front doorbell chime. Melissa didn't work Sundays, and she wasn't sure if

Damon had come in, so she ducked into her en suite, splashed water on her blotchy face and headed down the stairs to answer it.

Since leaving Damon in the garage, all she'd achieved was packing a couple of overnight bags. And a whole lot of crying. She'd expected him to follow her, to try and convince her to stay, and the fact he hadn't made a single move told her he was cooking up a plan to prevent her from leaving. Or he'd been called into work.

Either way, she was grateful for the time to pull herself together…to create a facade of someone who hadn't just had their world ripped out from under them.

She was in love with a man whose heart was black.

He'd as much as admitted it. *And* seen nothing wrong with the admission. The devastation went bone-deep. No, deeper—she could feel the ache in every cell of her body.

Tears formed again but she blinked them back. She had no choice, she had to leave. It'd been wrong to even consider the two-month trial, she could see that now.

This was never a love match.

So clinical, so cold. He was truly his uncle's nephew. And she wouldn't subject her baby or herself to a future of such emotional desolation.

The door chimed again as she swiped her hand over her cheeks, reached for the handle and opened. On the other side stood Travis Blakely's attorney.

"Crawford." Damon's deep voice came from behind her, sending a frisson of pure want through her system. She tensed every muscle in her body to rein in the impulses the want caused. She *would not* let this man— her husband—have sway over her.

Ian Crawford, briefcase in one hand, stood uneasily, eyes on Damon but darting frequently to Lily. "I need to speak to Mrs. Blakely for a moment."

Damon's arm snaked around her waist, holding her firm. "Then you'll speak to both of us."

She recognized the gesture for what it was—an act of propriety. The burn of resentment tamped down the desire his touch had caused. But she wouldn't fight him here and now, there was no need—as soon as this meeting was over, she was out the door.

Crawford gave a resigned sigh and nodded.

Damon stood back, bringing her with him, and let Crawford pass.

Lily watched the two men with their respective missions—Crawford to pass a private message from Travis, and Damon to prevent the secrecy. She had no energy to fight anymore, and looking at the set of Damon's strong shoulders, it'd be a waste of her time trying to speak to Crawford alone. Besides, Damon knowing wouldn't affect her actions or response. She might love him, but she was beyond considering his opinion in her decisions. He'd killed that.

She focused on the visitor, wanting to be polite and offer him a drink, but instead swallowed the question, needing this over with as much haste as she could arrange.

Crawford pursed his lips, the epitome of grim determination. "I won't take much of your time. I just need to deliver my message."

Damon nodded and led them into his formal living room.

Lily, reluctantly feeling like a hostess in Damon's

home, swept a hand toward a chair for Crawford and they all sat, she and Crawford on the edges of their chairs, Damon deep in his, seemingly unperturbed by the tension the others felt.

Lily clasped the silver heart pendant at her throat and asked, "You wanted to say something, Mr. Crawford?"

His eyes flicked from her to Damon and back again. "After you left, I'm afraid Mr. Blakely's condition deteriorated alarmingly—"

Her hand flew to her mouth. "He died?"

Crawford raised a hand to stop her thought. "No, but I don't believe that time is far away." He clasped his hands together on his lap before continuing. "He's been transferred to St. Rose's. He should be there by now."

Damon leaned forward, resting forearms on his thighs. "Yet you're here instead of by your master's side."

Crawford nodded, unmoved by the gibe. "He instructed me to come and ask a favor of your wife."

A favor? She saw Damon's posture tense at the same moment the apprehension descended over her. "What does he want?" she asked through numb lips.

Crawford pulled his briefcase onto his lap, clicked the lock then withdrew a typed page. "As you may have guessed, he doesn't expect to return home from this hospitalization." He paused as if waiting for his first point to sink in. "He has left a large house full of expensive contents vacant. He would like you, Mrs. Blakely, to reside in his home, and to do so without delay."

Live in that mausoleum? The thought sent a shiver across her skin. There was not a single aspect of a home about it. Despite having known it would pass to her baby, she hadn't considered the reality of living there so soon, before she'd had a chance to make it into a place fit for her child.

Damon scoffed a laugh. "The eyesore will hardly become derelict. He has a staff."

Crawford nodded. "Employees who need direction."

Lily's mind flew to the overnight bag, packed on her bed—she'd been thinking more of her empty rental house or her grandmother's home, not an enormous building of concrete and stone.

Damon leaned farther forward, toward their guest, in an action that looked almost intimidating. "If he's worried about the security risk, why ask a pregnant woman to stay there? Why not take safety measures? Hire a security guard."

Crawford coughed. "I'm sorry, I can't answer that. I'm simply acting on instructions from my client. This was not a decision I made." He held the piece of paper out to Lily. "He asked me to type up the request in case of future legal challenges, then he signed the bottom. His nurse witnessed the signature."

Damon arched a cynical brow. "He did all this in the midst of being transferred."

Crawford nodded. "He was quite determined."

"I bet he was," Damon muttered.

Lily skimmed the page and glanced at the signatures, the germ of an idea forming. Damon hated that house. It'd be the one place he wouldn't follow her—he'd told her more than once when they'd dated that he'd see it razed to the ground before living there again.

If she moved into her empty rental, chances were

he'd move in after her. And at her gran's…well, Damon would be welcomed like a long-lost son.

But he wouldn't stay in his childhood home, he'd made that clear in the past. She swallowed. Gaining physical distance from her husband was paramount. It was her only defense against his brutal methods of charm and seduction. Especially now she'd faced the reality that she loved him.

And if this house was to become her child's inheritance, then someone had to breathe some life into it first. It needed warmth and love before it was fit for her baby.

Fate may have dealt her this hand, but she'd make the most of it.

Damon surged to his feet, fists planted on narrow hips. "Just because Travis wants Lily to live there doesn't mean she will. You can take your—"

Lily stood and moved beside him, laying a hand on his forearm. "I'll do it," she said firmly.

A muscle ticked in Damon's jaw but before he could reply, Crawford closed his briefcase, dropped a set of keys in Lily's hand and headed for the door. "My number is on that letter with the offer. Let me know if you need anything." Then he all but ran from the house.

Damon narrowed his eyes, watching the retreat. "Coward." He swung toward her and fixed her with the intensity of his unflinching gaze. "You can't live there."

Lily gathered all her courage to face the immovability of Damon once he'd decided on a path. But she had to do this, for her very sanity. She raised her chin. "I can and I will. I told you I'm leaving."

Features controlled, he grasped her fingers and

brought their joined hands to rest on the muscled wall of his chest. "Lily, he's only doing this to make sure he's driven a wedge between us. He's using you to attack me. He'd do *anything* to hurt me."

The gall of his hypocrisy astounded her for a second, before she yanked her hand free. The pain of being insignificant to the man she loved beside his obsession with destruction slammed once again into her heart. "That sounds familiar," she hissed, barely restraining her anger. "I think someone else admitted that same fault recently—willing to do anything to hurt their 'enemy.'"

"This is different." The certainty in his ice-blue eyes reinforced that he had no understanding of how damaged his dark soul was.

Her shoulders slumped as all fight left her. "It doesn't matter. I don't care why he's done it, he has. And I'm moving."

She turned to the staircase. Being this close to the man who would never truly be hers was torture, as if a thousand jagged knives pierced her very soul.

She needed to get her bags and get out of here. And haste was an absolute priority. Every extra minute in his company added another unbearable blade to the relentless attack.

Damon stepped into her path, tall, solid, inflexible. "You were looking for an excuse to leave me," he accused, eyes narrowed. "You never had any intention of giving this marriage a real go—you had one foot out the door from the beginning."

She grimaced. How could he even need to ask this? "Because the foot inside the door was dragged there, not invited in. You bribed me into the vows. Moved my furniture to your room without my consent."

He didn't get it. Just didn't get it. And her heart squeezed painfully at the knowledge that he never would.

His expression changed and for the first time since Crawford's visit, honest emotion emerged in his eyes—need. "I don't want you to go," he rasped.

Too little, too late. "We don't always get what we want, Damon. And sometimes the only answer you can have is no."

She turned and ascended the staircase, catching a flash of the vulnerability on his face as she did. But she couldn't let herself worry about him anymore. She had to prepare for the move to her new home. Alone.

Eight

After two hours of packing and driving, Lily stepped into the foyer of Travis Blakely's mansion, a cold trickle of dread running through her veins. The old man's words had repeated over and over in her mind on the drive.

"Take care of the baby. Tell him about me."

Though it might sound absurd to people who had known and despised him, Lily wondered whether Travis, in his last days, had indeed caught a glimpse of what it truly meant to be human. Whether, after leading a manipulative, selfish existence, in the end he, too, had wanted to be loved or at least remembered. The little girl in her—the one who'd yearned for her parents to notice her, to want her—understood.

His actions to Damon were unforgivable; she could

never condone or excuse the damage he'd wreaked on the vulnerable child or the man Damon had become. But Gran's mantra had always been, hate the sin, love the sinner. It was how Gran had coped with her son's treatment of his own child, Lily. Gran had made sure Lily was no longer neglected, but she'd also made peace with her son in her heart long before his death.

Lily looked from the sweeping white marble staircase to the black-tiled ballroom entranceway—each facet of the decor reflected the coldness of its owner's heart.

Perhaps loving this sinner was too much to ask. But compassion? A little compassion she could spare for a fellow human being. Or try to.

And if you allow a drop of compassion for him, her heart whispered, *shouldn't you confer the same to his nephew?*

Instinctively, her hands went to her slightly rounded belly. No. As much as she'd like to forgive and trust Damon, she simply couldn't risk it. Access visits to their child when he was on his best, charming behavior was the limit of what she could afford. Constant contact would be a danger to the emotional well-being of both her and her child. She wouldn't allow anything to blur or erase that knowledge.

A plump man with a large walrus mustache shuffled toward her, interrupting her reverie. "Oh, Mrs. Blakely, we're glad you're here."

She'd always liked the man who acted as butler and chef rolled into one. There was a small staff to help, but Thomas ran this house.

She smiled for the first time in hours—since before she'd been summoned here earlier in the day…before she'd found out about the depths of the darkness in her husband's soul.

Even as she'd left and Damon had loaded the suitcase into her car, his silence had screamed his guilt. The proud jut of his jaw had broken away her last remnant of hope.

She took the last step toward the butler as he reached her. "Thomas, you're a sight for sore eyes."

He pulled her into a bear hug, something he'd never done before.

Confused, she allowed the hug, then pulled back. "Thomas?"

Eyebrows pinched together, he shuddered out a breath and shook his head. "We've had a call from the nurse. Mr. Blakely passed away fifteen minutes ago."

Lily felt the blood drain from her face. He'd died while she was driving to his house with his last words to her replaying in her mind. The hairs on the back of her neck stood on end.

At a lock clicking behind her, she and Thomas both turned to see Damon standing framed by the opened door, at his feet the suitcase she recognized from their trip to New Zealand.

"Honey, I'm home," he said with a wry smile.

Irritation surged that he'd followed her, but she had to acknowledge that part of her had known he would. Of course he would. And that same part of her wanted to be close to him, even now. To touch his solidness and be held.

But she pushed the tumult of emotions aside because, regardless of her physical reactions and his deplorable behavior, Damon's last immediate relative, besides their unborn baby, had just died.

How would he react to the news? Probably re-lieved—his contempt for his uncle would barely permit more, yet she couldn't be sure. She knew only that she needed to be the person to tell him.

Lily moved to his side and sought his eyes. "Damon, your uncle passed away a little while ago."

He stiffened, eyes boring into hers, but gave no clue to which emotion the news evoked.

Thomas moved forward. "If there's anything I can do…"

Damon's eyes flicked to Thomas. "No." He shook his head, as if shaking off a passing mood. "You probably had more affection for him than anyone, Thomas, and I know that wasn't much. I'm well aware he had to pay for your loyalty."

Thomas shrugged, a confused sadness in his eyes. "He wasn't an easy man to work for, but I won't speak ill of the dead."

Damon gave a curt nod. "Tell the others that regard-less of what happens with the estate, I'll make sure they're taken care of."

Lily held back a gasp. *He'd* take care of them? It was her place, surely, to take care of the house and its inhabi-tants? But she held back the words as they balanced on her lips. Of course Damon would think this way. And for many reasons, it wasn't the time to start arguments. She'd let it slide this once.

But just this once—she was through having her life dictated by Damon Blakely.

"Thank you." Thomas began to say more, blinked, closed his mouth then walked away.

Once they were alone, Damon thrust his hands into his pockets and looked around. "I guess this is all yours, sweetheart."

She wrapped her arms around herself in a futile attempt to ward off the ugliness of the whole situation. It seemed too cold to be calculating a dead man's assets so soon after his passing. "I'm not comfortable talking about this yet."

He let out a scornful laugh. "Come on, Lily. Don't tell me you're mourning that despot."

"No…not really. It's just…within a few hours, I've been lobbed into this house and a fortune—" *and heard the truth about the man I love and his view of me and our marriage* "—I guess I feel…actually, I don't know *how* I feel."

"Understandable. But it doesn't change the fact that you've inherited all my uncle's assets."

She looked up, searching his face for hidden meaning. "I told you I'd share it with you."

He shook his head in slow, almost methodical movements. "It's all yours. I only ever wanted BlakeCorp."

Lily felt her jaw slacken. Was he serious? "I thought you'd want it all, or at least half. Even Travis expected court battles."

"Perhaps Travis didn't know me as well as he thought he did." He raised one eyebrow and the implication hung in the air, that she'd unfairly judged him, too.

Had she? Discovering that Damon had been waging a war of destruction against his uncle without her even suspecting had shown her many things, including the more she knew about Damon, the less she knew about him.

If you allow a drop of compassion for Travis, her heart repeated, *shouldn't you confer the same to his nephew?*

Yet…Damon seemed to live for acquisitions. "Even if you hate the house, you still must have expected it'd come to you?"

He shrugged, seemingly unconcerned. "This property is small peanuts. My portfolio is worth more than ten times what Travis was at his peak. A house here or there barely registers."

She frowned and watched him walk back to his luggage, bring it in and close the door. Could it be that simple? A mere issue of sums and figures, with no consideration of Damon's driving force—ownership. Possession. Retribution.

If there was more to this laying down of his sword, he wasn't ready to share details. She could see that from the set of his shoulders. The closed angles of his face. He'd spring the surprise of his true motives on her at some stage…but this time, she'd be expecting it.

Damon was only generous when it suited his purpose. He'd taught her that well.

She wrapped a hand around her throat, knowing it was a defensive move even as she made it. "However we do it, I consider my portion belongs to our baby. And that's only if there are no challenges to the will."

He waved a hand, tossing the idea aside. "I'm the only one who'd have a claim to challenge. And I told you I won't. It's yours." He moved over to a hall table and picked up a crystal bowl in casual assessment. "Will you sell?"

"No." She swallowed convulsively. "There was some

fine print in his will that I only noticed when Crawford's letter pointed it out. I can't sell. I only inherit if I keep it so it can be passed to the baby in turn."

Replacing the bowl, he stretched his arms wide, taking in the interior of his childhood home. "So rent it out. Leave it here to rot." He lifted one shoulder then dropped it in a nonchalant gesture of disinterest. "Let the Dog Protection Society use it as kennels. But don't live in it. It's as cold as a coffin."

"I have to." Her voice wavered and she cursed it. This wasn't something she needed to be anxious about. She had a plan.

He turned back to face her, eyes trained on hers. "Why?"

She took a breath, held it, then released it slowly. "That was the rest of the fine print. I inherit only if I don't sell, and I live in it for at least twelve months."

Damon swore. "Then forfeit. Nothing is worth that."

"I wouldn't just lose the house. I'd lose everything. The money. BlakeCorp. Everything." She couldn't do it to her baby or Gran, or even Damon, despite what he'd done. They might have no future, but she wouldn't be another person to deny him his birthright. "It'd all go to your cousin, Mark."

He held her gaze, unmoving, face impassive, and a vague cloud of suspicion filtered through her mind. Why didn't he react to the possibility of losing Blake-Corp? His lack of concern didn't make sense. But before she could make any meaning of the thought, Damon closed the distance between them.

He took her hands, gripping firmly. "Travis is trying

to flex his muscle from beyond the grave." His jaw hardened. "We can't let him win."

For several seconds, she soaked up his touch, his nearness, his heat, before stepping back, out of his reach. "I have no intention of letting him win. I'm going to beat him at his own game."

His forehead wrinkled in disbelief. "By doing what he tells you?"

"No. By making this old place a home." A place of stability and security that could never be taken away. No one could gamble away her child's clothes and toys. No one would force her child to move on before she or he even made friends or settled into school. No one would ever have that power again.

She crossed her arms under her breasts, holding the thought close to her heart. "I can make it something worth inheriting." And then, despite the maneuverings of Travis, she'd have had the last say in the whole affair.

Damon regarded her with an expression bordering on pity. "This house is a lost cause." He extended a hand. "Come home with me."

Lily took a step back. She had her plan worked out. She'd be independent, a home owner. And no one, *no one,* would ever again use her as a pawn for their own ends—by buying a stake in a poker match, or marrying her to access a will—again. She squared her shoulders and met his gaze. "I'll transform it. Make it into a home. Don't worry about me, I want to be here."

He stepped closer, following her retreat, and cupped her shoulders. "I'm not leaving you and our baby alone at night waiting for thieves, or worse. By morning the world will know Travis Blakely is dead and it's no secret the contents of this place are valuable. It may have been an excuse for getting you here, but Travis was right about that. I won't leave you vulnerable."

A shudder ran down her spine at the thought of being in this cold house late at night, pregnant, alone but for staff at the other end of the building. She'd likely lie awake listening to every little bump and creak. To know Damon was down the hall…she'd be safe.

But after breaking up with him, she couldn't ask it. She licked dry lips. "The house has an elaborate security system. And three live-in staff. If it was enough to protect a sick, dying man, it'll be enough to protect me."

Damon's mouth set in a grim line. "If you're staying, then so am I." He retraced his steps to the door and picked up his luggage. "We'll take the main bedroom in the north wing."

Lily sat on the edge of the bed in the south-wing bedroom she'd moved to. She'd changed into a satin lilac nightgown and was ready to turn in, but something stopped her.

Restless, she crossed to the dresser, picked up a sheaf of papers and began to flick through the plans she'd sketched for the revamping of the mansion. She'd had the ideas and hadn't wanted to waste time, so had asked Thomas to bring her a tray instead of going down for dinner. The side benefit was avoiding another confrontation with Damon over the dinner table.

Damon. At the thought of him, her restlessness escalated and her blood heated. Thinking of the way the warmth of his hands could suffuse the fabric of her clothes to warm her right through. The seductive timbre of his voice. Memories of the hot slide of naked bodies in the dark of night.

Her core throbbed and her skin tingled with awareness. How would she go through her life, never lying with him again? Never rising to the heights that only he could take her?

And yet she *couldn't* give in to her body's insistent clamoring for his lovemaking. She had to keep her distance. They'd been down this path before and it led to heartbreak….

So why, she asked herself, was her hand on the doorknob?

She let out a long sigh. If she were completely honest, she had to admit something, even if only to herself. She wanted Damon with a blinding need. He was down the hall. He was her husband. And it didn't *have* to mean anything. Didn't have to mean they had a future.

The morning after they'd arrived back in Australia, married, he'd said maybe all that mattered was how right it felt when they made love, and they'd handle the aftermath when it happened.

Come. Live in the moment with me, he'd said.

Her eyes drifted closed as she contemplated sneaking into his room, climbing under the covers, perhaps finding him naked, welcoming her. The vision left her light-headed with craving.

Maybe she could live in the moment just once more….

Pulse racing, Lily opened the door and padded silently down the hall. She'd regret this tomorrow, but right now the need to touch him, to be touched, was something she could no longer deny or control.

She paused outside his door and took a long breath. How would Damon react to this late-night visit? Would he be self-satisfied that she'd come to him? Read more into it than it meant? Leaning her forehead against the door, her body yearning for him, she realized it made no difference how he reacted. She needed him.

She turned the knob quietly and edged the door open enough to slip through. Damon lay sprawled on the four-poster bed against a pile of pillows, bare chested, with a glass of red wine in one hand and the other arm up behind his head. His eyes were closed but his body was too tense for him to be asleep. A soft light spilled from a lamp, shrouding him in its golden glow and leaving most of the room in shadows.

At the sharp click as she closed the door, his eyes flashed open. His face was a picture of surprised wonderment. Within moments he'd taken in the scene, put his wine on a side table and was at her side, drawing her tightly against him. Lily trembled with want now he was holding her, now she could feel his body against hers.

"Thank God," he whispered into her hair. "I was about two seconds away from knocking on your door."

Her breath hitched at the deep rumble of his voice, but she made herself speak, to say it. "Damon, this doesn't mean—"

He leaned down, his warm breath caressing her ear as he kept her tightly enfolded against his body. "Shh."

"I just had to be in your arms again," she said, her

voice almost a sob. She reached out and twined her hands behind his neck, wanting him closer still. "In your bed."

His hands traced a path down her sides, skimming the satin nightdress, curving over her hips. "I know."

The familiar melting of her body from the inside out was as potent as it was welcome. Needing to touch him, to taste him, she pressed a kiss to his bare chest and he groaned.

"Lily, I want you so badly I can barely remember who I am."

Slowly, too slowly for her, he lowered his mouth and his lips whispered across hers. Burning for him, she raised herself onto her toes to hurry the kiss, then felt her entire body soften as he granted her request.

His lips were hungry, confident, moving over hers with such heat that she opened to him and welcomed his tongue, welcomed his teeth on her bottom lip, welcomed whatever he would do. He tasted of sweet wine and passion and she skimmed her hands over the solid muscles of his chest, up over his strong shoulders, along his back.

Just when her head began to swim, Damon pulled away, leaving them both trying to catch their breath. Their eyes met in silence, and for one moment reason broke through the fog of desire in her mind. Was this wrong? Was she making things between them more complicated? More difficult to walk away from?

Then he held out his hand and she couldn't have resisted taking it for all the world. If they had no future, then she'd give herself this gift—one night of memories to sustain her through the nights without him.

"Come with me," he said, tugging on her hand. He led her to the side of the bed, reached down for the glass of wine and lifted it to her lips. She sipped as he tilted the glass, and she felt the rich, mellow fluid slide down her throat. Then he held her gaze as he sipped from the same glass. Something about sharing the wine with him made her heart clench, as if the gesture held some deeper meaning.

He replaced the glass on the side table and smoothly lifted her nightdress over her head. The cold air nipped at her skin, contrasting with the burning heat inside her. Needing him more than air, she reached out.

"Just let me look at you for a moment," Damon rasped. He stepped away from her, his eyes feasting on her naked body the way patrons at the gallery might look at a masterpiece.

Her skin erupted in gooseflesh wherever his eyes rested, and she felt a thrill of power in her own body, felt beautiful in his eyes.

"You're the most exquisite thing I've seen in my life." Damon moved closer and she breathed him in— the woody, musky clean scent of him.

He took her left hand and guided it to the glass of wine, then he dipped her fingers into the bowl before lifting them to his mouth. Two droplets of the deep red wine dripped onto his chest before he caught her fingertips between his lips. He circled them with his tongue, nipping gently then sucking firmly. As if a direct line connected her fingers to her core, a tug of molten heat arrowed its way through her body and she moaned.

"Damon," she breathed, her eyes drifting closed.

"Let me worship your body tonight."

Her eyes opened and she saw the promise in his eyes. "Yes. God, yes."

The droplets of wine on his chest had run a little, leaving a moist trail down his solid muscles. With barely a thought, she leaned in and ran her tongue along the path, tasting the richness of the wine, mixed with the taste of Damon's skin. Ambrosia, the food of the gods, could hold no more delight than this. All traces of the wine gone, she moved lower, tasting the skin over the ridges of his abdomen. His breath caught as she nipped, so she did it again.

His hands cupped her face and he brought her back up to meet his eyes. "Have mercy, sweetheart."

He kissed her—soft, slow and mind-blowing—bringing her closer, closer, till their bodies were pressed together. Knees like jelly, she wavered, but he held her tightly and she knew she'd never fall while he held her. How could a relationship between them be so wrong when they felt like *this* together?

With one arm supporting her, he reached across to whip the covers from the bed before lifting her and laying her across the crisp cotton sheets. Lily almost cried in bliss, knowing there was nowhere else on earth she'd rather be than in Damon's bed. Her husband's bed.

He parted her thighs and knelt between them. The vision of him leaning over her body, strong and potent, made her pulse spike. But his trousers sitting low on his hips interrupted the picture. "Have you forgotten something?" she whispered.

A corner of his sensual mouth curved. "If I take them

off, I might be tempted to take you too soon. And I want to spend much longer than that here with you."

"But I need the feel of you in my hand." She reached down to caress the hardness straining against his zipper. "Can I touch you?"

Muscles bunched across his shoulders, his chest tensed, his breathing quickened. But he rasped, "Yes."

She undid the buckle on his belt and drew it from the loops of his trousers then let it fall to the floor. A fiery need raced through her and she reached down with both hands to cup him through the fabric again, stroking. He lifted his tense body higher, up onto his toes and fists that rested either side of her shoulders.

"Lily," he groaned, then bent his head down, body still held inches above hers, and claimed her mouth.

This kiss was more greedy than the first, more demanding, more raw. He turned his head, changing the angle, and her hands slid away from his trousers, up his sides to his back, and she was helpless to do more than cling to him.

With one quick motion, without breaking the kiss, he rolled, bringing her on top of him, holding her firm against his body. The full-length contact was what she'd been craving since she'd left her bedroom, and now that she had it, a soft sigh escaped her lips. She moved, rubbing her breasts across the coarse hair of his chest, rubbing her hips against his despite the fabric in their way.

She reached for the zipper, but he caught her wrist.

"Before you slipped through my door tonight," he said, breathing hard from their kiss, "I was lying here, thinking of the things I wanted to do to you. Like this, for example." With hands gripping her sides, he lifted her torso high, arching her back, then he captured the peak of one breast in his hot mouth. He gently abraded with his teeth as he pulled with his lips, and sparks shot out from her nerve endings, flooding her body until she was limp and would have fallen but for his strong hands holding her in the air.

"Damon, I'm not sure how much longer I can stand that." She squeezed the words out as she reached to run hands through his thick dark hair.

"Then I'll stop," he said easily. Too easily. With barely time for her to catch her breath, he found the peak of her other breast and began the same sweet torture.

She bucked her hips against his, mindless, and heard his groan. He rolled them again, so she lay beneath him and he pinned her to the bed.

Looking up into his ice-blue eyes, now darker with desire, she felt her heart swell with the love for him she normally kept leashed. Tears pricked the backs of her eyes and her throat felt thick. "Damon, whatever else happens, I want you to know this is real between us. This connection we have is real and precious to me."

He kissed her tenderly. "It's precious to me, too."

He reached for the wine and, gently wrapping his arm behind her shoulders, lifted so she could sip from the glass he placed against her lips. Then, eyes locked on hers, he sipped as well. Her heart almost stopped beating with the power of the gesture; it was as if they'd toasted the importance, the honesty of their connection. He might never love her, but this was almost as good. Almost.

Damon reared back from her and allowed three, then four droplets of wine to fall into her belly button. With her skin sensitized, each droplet made her gasp.

He replaced the glass on the side table, then edged down the bed, to lick the wine from her stomach. "Making love to you has always been best when it's a little messy," he said with a lazy grin.

A delicious shiver ran down her spine as memories crowded into her mind, competing with the current sensations. "I remember the picnic at that secluded spot near the falls."

"Mango slices, dripping juice," he added as his hands trailed down along her thighs, before splaying them over her hips.

"I thought I'd pass out from the intensity that day," she whispered.

His smooth moist tongue explored farther across her slightly rounded belly, before he paused and laid a tender kiss on her abdomen. Then he moved lower still, and when his tongue plunged in the most intimate of kisses, she cried out his name.

She writhed below him, but his hands trapped her hips firmly, keeping her in place. Her muscles were melting, her bones—everything—dissolving. The only reality that remained was his mouth and its rhythmic movements. Nothing else existed. His hands slid up to her breasts to gently flick the peaks, and she truly broke free of the world, crying his name, racing higher, until she imploded and floated in a place where nothing existed beyond Damon and the way he made her body come alive.

Vaguely she felt him move to her side and pull her into an embrace that felt like home. After timeless moments she opened her eyes to find him staring at her, a puzzled line on his forehead.

She snuggled closer. "Why the frown?"

He absently stroked her side. "I'm trying to work out why every time we make love, it's better than the time before. Why I've never had enough. I always need you more."

A discussion of their marriage was the last thing she needed now. Or philosophizing on how her decision to come here tonight would impact on their future.

So instead she kept it light. "I think some things are beyond explaining." And she reached for his trousers. This time he let her unzip him and push the trousers and boxers to his ankles before he maneuvered them off to fall on the floor.

She reached to cup him again, the way she had through the fabric, but this time there was no barrier. She stroked with one hand, whisper soft, then bent to kiss the hardness.

"Lily." The word was wrenched from his throat. "You'll kill me, you know that?" He pulled her up for a quick, hard kiss, then edged off the bed to stand before her, and her heart missed a beat at the sight of his masculine beauty.

He held out his hands, but she hesitated. She'd wanted this, had come to his room in the dead of night for this, but now the culmination of her fantasy was here, she wanted to delay it. Couldn't bear it to end.

"Take my hand, sweetheart," he said softly, and smiled into her eyes.

Without another thought she reached for his out-stretched hands and he pulled her to her feet, lifting her high against him until her toes no longer touched the ground and all thoughts fled. She wrapped her legs around his waist, buried her hands in his hair.

In a haze of passion, she draped him with her body, her fingers curling and unfurling in his hair. She could feel his heart beating powerfully against her chest, his hands shifting her hips to increase the pleasure for them both.

He lowered himself to sit on the edge of the bed, the slide of skin on skin as he brought her to straddle him sending shivers up her spine. Then he lifted her again, and brought her down onto him. She felt herself expand to embrace him, rocked a little to fully appreciate the sensation.

"You said this was real and precious, Lily?" He moved in her and her breath caught. "It's more than that. It's everything."

Not wanting to confirm his meaning, she said against his mouth, "Just keep going." He shifted his hips, rocked them both higher, and she gasped.

"Lily, this is right," he said, an edge of torment in his voice. He raked his hands down her back, then wrapped them tightly around her, increasing the friction against her breasts as he moved higher in her. "We belong together."

A single tear slid down her cheek. He was right. The sensations he created in her were so beautiful, how could she have thought she could live without this? Everything else would work out. It had to.

"Yes," she whispered into his ear. "This is right."

Something like a growl rumbled in his chest and he

moved faster, higher. She reached out to brace one hand on a corner bedpost, the other hand woven in his hair, her eyes locked on Damon's.

As the power built inside her, she bit down on her lip, trying to hold on, to extend this moment of perfection as long as she could. Her grip on the post tightened, her whole body thrummed until she flew high enough to join the stars and she let go of the post and everything else, feeling Damon convulse and follow her out into the cosmos.

Nine

Lily woke in her husband's light-filled bedroom, a sleepy smile easing across her face. She stretched and reached for Damon.

The sheets were cold where his body had lain during the night. Sitting up, she looked for him, listened for sounds of the shower from the en suite, but there was nothing. A familiar ache touched her chest, but she ignored it. She'd been the one to slip into his room last night. Had gone willingly to his bed with no expectations beyond the pleasure they could bring each other. He had a right to his own movements this morning.

From the corner of her eye she saw a slip of paper on his pillow and reached for it.

"Sweetheart, I have to go into the office, but I'll be home as soon as I can. D"

Lily smiled ruefully at herself. Of course he'd gone to work. She should have predicted it.

She found her nightdress and quickly made her way down the hall to her own bedroom. During her shower, flashes of the night before filled her senses. The feel of Damon's hands on her body. The taste of his skin. The sound he made deep in his throat when he found release.

She shut off the faucet and, mind still pleasurably full of Damon, she toweled off and pulled on clothes. As she slipped on her sandals the phone rang, jolting her from the memories. She debated leaving it for Thomas, but since she was standing beside her room's extension, she picked up.

A thin, nervous voice asked, "Mrs. Blakely?"

"Good morning, Mr. Crawford."

"Oh, good. I'm glad you're home. I've discovered some rather disturbing information and wondered if I could call around to talk to you about it."

Her pulse spiked. *Disturbing information* were two words she didn't want to hear from her lawyer. "I'd rather you told me now."

"The thing is, I'm unsure of how much you already know. It's of a delicate nature."

Frowning, Lily leaned back onto the bedpost. Now the disturbing news was delicate, as well. "All I know is what you and Travis have told me."

Crawford cleared his throat. "Perhaps you should sit down."

"Please, just tell me."

He took a deep breath and hesitated before continuing. "As Travis Blakely's executor, I've been looking into his holdings before passing them on. It seems there were many things he didn't share with me or his other attorneys."

Her nails curled into her palms as she sank onto the bed. "What did you find?"

"Travis Blakely was not in possession of the assets that he willed to you."

Not in possession of the assets. The words reverberated in her head and she pressed a hand to her chest, attempting to quell her racing heart. "The house? The money?"

"He had nothing," Crawford said sympathetically, as if attempting to soften the blow. "Worse than nothing—the estate owes money in missed payments on loans."

A quick rush of panic rose to encircle her throat. "He left me a debt? I'm in debt!" Her voice sounded unnaturally high in her ears. She'd lost her independence. Her security. Her baby's security. She dropped her head into her free hand and focused on keeping her lungs breathing while all her plans dissolved into thin air.

"There's more."

Her head jerked up as adrenaline surged through her bloodstream. More? What more could there possibly be? She straightened and braced herself for worse. "Go on."

"The assets and holdings that Travis Blakely thought he owned were acquired by various companies. I've only been able to follow the complicated trail on some of them so far, and those lead back to one person. I suspect once I've traced the others back they'll end up at the same person as well."

Her heart clenched tight and she *knew.* "Damon." As

she said his name aloud, acknowledged what she knew to be true, her stomach fell away.

Crawford coughed nervously. "He really hasn't told you any of this?"

Not a word. She gripped the bedpost as her head began to spin. *Not even a hint.* She swallowed and waited until her throat relaxed enough to speak. "What do we do from here?"

"I still have quite a bit of work to do, but when I'm finished, I'll give you a full report, including the steps that need to be taken."

"Thank you, Mr. Crawford." Lily hung up with a shaky hand and closed her eyes.

He'd lied to her. He'd stood there in the foyer last night and discussed what she could do with this house, when he already owned it.

Had anything between them ever been real? The tender moments they'd shared... Him staying with her in this mansion to ensure her safety... The love they'd made last night... She gripped the silver heart on her necklace as she attempted to settle nausea that had nothing to do with her pregnancy.

And this house—the one she'd planned to make over as a permanent place of stability for her and her child—didn't belong to her. Damon had somehow acquired it.

Her legs trembled and felt weak, but she made herself stand. She had to leave. Cut ties with Damon. Now. It was unthinkable to remain here with a man who could so blatantly lie to her.

Betray her.

Burning tears filled her eyes, but she refused to acknowledge them. Instead she summoned the inner strength that had sustained her through a childhood with erratic parents.

Leaving the man who'd betrayed her as she'd never been betrayed before was the right thing to do for herself, but more important, for her baby.

She had to go.

Lily sat on a russet wingback in the mansion's formal library, feet tucked up under her, hands clenched together on her lap. On the verge of emotional exhaustion. It had been three hours since Crawford had delivered the bombshell that had shattered her heart—her life—and her bags were packed and in the car. Now she only waited for her husband to arrive.

Since Damon had rung to say he was leaving work early, she'd been on tenterhooks, alternating between sitting on this chair and restlessly toying with books on the floor-to-ceiling shelves. Her whole body was taut, like a rubber band ready to snap, but she'd forced herself to bide her time before she could confront her husband about his betrayal.

Then she must leave.

An excruciating pain stabbed her heart at the thought, but she pushed the pain aside. There would be time enough to grieve later.

The crunch of wheels over the driveway's polished gravel announced his arrival. Wanting to meet her fate head-on despite the heavy bands constricting her lungs, the pounding in her head, she rose and walked to the foyer. She listened with hyperfocus to his car door open and close. His steps on the walkway seemed to echo the thudding beat of her heart.

The door opened, then he was there, in the marble foyer with her, dominating the space. Her body was drawn by their magnetic connection even now; her heart cried out for him.

But she couldn't listen.

He walked over and dropped a kiss on her cheek. "Are you waiting to welcome me home?" he asked, a teasing note in his voice.

She swallowed, lifted her chin. "I'm waiting for you, yes."

It had started to drizzle outside—she could see the fine droplets in his dark hair and on his suit coat. Part of her wanted to shake her fingers through the waves of his hair to rid him of the raindrops, the way a wife might lovingly nurture her husband. But her love for Damon had always been her Achilles' heel.

Their marriage was irrevocably broken. He'd stood in this very foyer yesterday and lied to her about something as important as their child's home. Her hands slid to her gently rounded belly and she took a small step back.

Damon seemed to take in her mood and frowned. "What's wrong, sweetheart?"

"I know—" Her voice wobbled to a stop. She took another breath. "I know about your…scheme."

Wary now, Damon set his briefcase down, rested his hands on his hips. "My scheme?"

She gripped the silver heart on her necklace and found a strong, even voice. "I had a call from Crawford today."

He winced and muttered an oath. "What did he tell you?"

Lily felt her jaw slacken, all traces of anguish over this confrontation gone in an instant. How very Blakely of him. His first response wasn't to come clean. Wasn't to beg her forgiveness. It was a damage assessment. Her blood heated at the calculated way his heart and mind worked, even when the stakes were so high.

She looked him square in the eye. "How about we start with this house. The one *you* own."

He reached for her hand, but she took another step back, refusing to allow him that intimacy.

"Lily, I'm sorry you found out." His voice had changed, become less confident. "I never meant for you to know."

She shook her head, incredulous. "You're not sorry for lying to me? Just that you got caught? I think I need to—"

"Lily, let me explain." His eyes—his whole face—were uncertain, exposed, and that shocked her almost as much as finding out she didn't own a single thing.

She crossed her arms under her breasts, trying desperately to protect her heart from his display of vulnerability. To keep this man's sins at the forefront of her mind, how he'd callously taken every opportunity to stick the knife in his uncle's back, had disregarded her choices at every turn.

"You have ten minutes to explain how you have the deed, Damon."

She marched through the archway, then turned sharply to face him, beyond caring that he'd see her ragged breathing. "You can start now."

He sat heavily in one of the russet wingbacks, leaning over to rest his forearms on his knees. Then he looked up and captured her gaze. "I've been buying my uncle's assets since I was twenty. Travis made it ridiculously easy by taking out loans he couldn't afford and not telling his lawyers. Greed and arrogance left him drastically overextended, so I've been using dummy companies to call in the loans."

She closed her eyes briefly. Of course he had. Damon schemed and manipulated situations as second nature— why hadn't she guessed he'd already claimed back everything he thought Travis owed him? She sank into the other wingback, summoning her reserves of courage to ask for the details. "Travis knew about two companies. No one knew about the rest?"

Damon shook his head slowly, eyes not leaving hers. "I was waiting until I had everything before I told him. Everything he thought he owned—even Blake-Corp—is mine."

"Why?" Though she asked the question, she already knew the answer. She needed to hear it from him, to hear it all.

He shrugged one shoulder. "The lure of destroying him, the same way he tried to destroy me, was too strong. I've been working toward this for years, and now…" His voice trailed off.

Revenge. *It was all about revenge.*

Knowing Travis, she understood Damon's thirst for vengeance, but she could never condone it. "And now he's dead and you can't gloat." To her own ears, her voice was flat, as empty as she felt inside.

He closed his eyes, looking almost sick, or despairing. "No, that's *not* it." He swallowed hard. "I want you to keep the house."

Lily almost smiled. How noble. But she didn't need his house, or his housekeeper, or his nanny, or his millions. She never had. Another thing he'd failed to understand about her. From early in life she'd learned to make it on her own, and heaven knew she could make it on her own now. She'd look after herself, Gran and the baby.

She waved away his regret with a flick of her wrist and instead focused on the question pounding through her brain. "You didn't think, at *any* time since you proposed, to tell me about this? Even when I told you Travis had changed his will?"

His hands curled over, then he released them. "I couldn't undermine your security—I know what it means to you. You need to feel stable, and I was giving it to you."

She gasped. Was he insane? By letting her live a lie, he hadn't just undermined any sense of stability, he'd utterly destroyed it.

She set her jaw. "You underestimated me. I could have coped with losing the security—I've bounced back from worse." Her father had ripped it out from under her often enough. "But I'll *never* forgive you for betraying me with the lies all this time."

He moved smoothly over to grab one of her hands. "All of this means nothing. We're still going to have a baby, we're still going to be a family."

Lily's heart skipped a beat and she suddenly felt faint

as the reality of what he hadn't said hit home. He didn't love her. He never had or could. He still held on to too much hurt.

And even though her heart bled for his troubled soul, she wouldn't fall for his empty words. They were a pretty illusion, a means to an end.

"Don't bother, Damon. You couldn't say a single thing that would make me believe you have any feelings for me but ownership."

She was so choked up she could barely get the words out. "So the house is yours. Enjoy it." Where would she go? It didn't matter, as long as it was far from the need to control still shining from his eyes.

She took a step toward the hall entrance, but Damon moved to block her path with the solidness of his body.

"My attorney will be in touch to tell you when the baby is born and to discuss visitation rights." She stepped around him and headed for the hall, feeling as if she might be sick.

"Lily, you can't leave."

The gravel-edged rasp in his voice made her turn in time to see his face distort with grief. But she couldn't let herself believe it; she had to protect herself and her baby.

She walked straight into the hall, picked up her keys on the way and continued outside. The blood rushed past her ears so loudly she could barely hear anything else.

Damon had been right about one thing. The house was full of torment. But it wasn't in the walls. It was in the hearts and minds of the Blakely men. She would never let him have sway over her again, or warp her baby's mind into the Blakely way of life.

Ten

Damon sat in his Lexus in the art gallery car park, unfamiliar nerves squirming in his belly. Lily was just inside those doors. His wife. It had been two whole weeks since he'd seen her and, God above, he wanted her. Wanted her in his bed. Talking to him. With him during the day. Holding his hand. Everything. Just *her*. So much, he ached with it. He couldn't wait to see her hold their baby, to nurse it and bring a smile to its cherubic face.

But—he scrubbed his hands across his face—he couldn't let himself get carried away with fantasy just yet or he might lose her for good. Lose their future.

His gut clenched and swooped at the memory of her walking out the door, walking away from him. He knew now he needed to lay the blame for ruining their marriage at his own door, and it tied him in knots knowing he'd hurt her. A beautiful soul like hers was a rare treasure. Priceless.

He also knew she might never forgive him for the deception, and that was a risk he had to take. Having her pure heart in his life unquestionably made him a better man. He'd done his damn best in the past two weeks to make things up to her, and now it was time to show her the results of that work.

His pulse spiked at the thought of seeing her again. Her smile swam before his eyes, her scent surrounded him. The silken feel of her long hair made his hands twitch. He craved the feel of her skin under his fingertips, needed to have her sweet lips touch his. *Love?* Such a small and inadequate word. He was *drowning* in the depth of need and want he felt for her.

Why hadn't he realized before that he loved her? He dragged in a lungful of air and held it, trying to steady his breathing. He had no idea when he'd fallen in love with her. All he knew was he'd fallen harder than he'd thought possible.

And now it was time to show her how much.

Lily stood from her desk and stretched. Needing a break from the paperwork that had taken most of her morning, she strolled down the corridor of the gallery's office section.

As she walked, her hands moved to a familiar position—across her rounded stomach—and her thoughts drifted to her baby. And her baby's father.

Her pulse picked up at the mere thought of him,

despite all he'd done. Worse still was the ache in her heart. She missed him with every fiber of her being. Each time the baby moved she wanted to put his hand on her belly, to share it. When she had news, she wanted to call him, to hear his voice filled with warm congratulation or gentle comfort. She even missed the things he'd done for her—high-handed, yes, but done because he wanted to make her life easier....

And she missed his touch. Not just sexual, though God knew that was constant—she missed his smile, the way he'd look at her, or hold her hand.

The little things.

But she hated that weakness. She needed to settle the financial mess between them, and make arrangements for their baby's future. What was best for her unborn child had to be her *only* consideration. Divorce was definitely a priority. She couldn't possibly get over him while she was his wife.

She wandered into an exhibition on Indian Art. The space looked beautiful with the choices of artwork the curator, her friend Robyn, had made, and the swathes of fabric draped around columns. Too gorgeous to dismantle in a week. Yet it was temporary, as her whole life seemed to be. Maybe always would be. She'd really believed the house Travis had left her would be the start of a new phase of permanence. And, despite repeated evidence to the contrary, that small kernel of hope that Damon could be a part of that stable future had refused to be squashed.

Would she ever learn?

From the corner of her eye she saw a man in a crisp

tailored suit, his hair a shade darker than midnight. All the air in her lungs squeezed out as she turned to watch Damon stride toward her. His gaze intent on her, hungry and…and yes, in *pain*. His long legs strode across the room, eyes locked on hers, as if he saw nothing but her, *wanted* nothing but her.

She struggled to fill her oxygen-starved lungs.

In his hand was a single page that he fidgeted with— she'd never seen him restless before. Something must be wrong. Or perhaps he needed her signature on some business document. That must be why he'd come.

Feeling unsteady, as if she was about to fall from a cliff, she took the last steps to meet him.

It took tensing every muscle she had to stop from throwing herself into his arms—but that was ridiculous, she shouldn't feel that way. She would stay strong to her last breath. She had to.

She nodded politely. "Hello, Damon."

She saw it again…a discernible difference in his eyes—that raw emotion she thought she'd glimpsed moments ago. Pain, regret, yearning. And still he didn't speak. She clasped her perspiring hands together. Oh, God, something *was* wrong.

"What is it? What's happened?"

He shook his head sharply, as if waking from a dream. "You. You've happened."

Confused, aching to touch him, she forced herself to step back. She'd been tricked before when her body had proven itself untrustworthy. She had to think with her head and forget about her heart.

Her chin kicked up even as her knees threatened to

buckle. "You're not making any sense. What do you mean, *I've* happened?"

Expression neutral, he said, "I've come to show you something. Come with me." He extended a hand.

Yes. Even her palm burned to have the connection. Her hand began to lift before she tucked it tightly under her breasts with the other. "I'm not following you anywhere, Damon. And I'm not touching you."

He gave a wry imitation of a smile and dropped his hand. "Of course." He held out the page he carried.

She kept her arms tightly crossed. "What's that?"

He quirked an eyebrow as if he had nothing to hide, as if he was the most trustworthy man on earth. "Read it," he said, "and you'll see."

Lily bit down on her lip. She couldn't think of anything Damon could show her that would make a difference. And yet, she couldn't help but be drawn to this unusual aura he was exuding. If appearances were enough, she might almost be convinced that he'd turned over that new leaf. Where was the seductive charm, the manipulative gleam in his eye?

She held herself tighter.

It had been difficult to say no to him before. Today it was near impossible.

Curiosity piqued and, heart drawn to him, she bit her lip again and finally relented. "Okay, but I'll warn you now it won't make a difference."

He smiled, genuinely this time, and she marveled at how that expression transformed his face into something as breathtaking as a master's Grecian sculpture. "Your warning is duly noted."

She took the page and skimmed the words. It was a flyer for a new gallery; a privately owned gallery open to the public. Owned by…her grandmother!

"Would you like me to take you there?" His jaw tightened, as though readying himself to argue her refusal.

What was he up to? She raised her head to meet his ice-blue eyes. Had Damon turned to manipulating Gran?

She hardened her heart. "What have you done?"

"Something different—no games, I swear." His eyes were clear, somber. "Let me show you. Can you get the afternoon off?"

Since she'd last seen him she'd accumulated more than enough overtime to cover an afternoon. The question was whether she wanted to be pulled back into one of his schemes. But if Gran was involved, Lily had to make sure it was all aboveboard. She'd never let anyone hurt Gran.

Watching him, she felt the familiar pull of arousal and struggled against it. It had betrayed her before. He couldn't be genuine. Couldn't be.

Could he?

Hating herself for giving in, she gave a brisk nod. "I'll meet you in the car park in ten minutes."

She rushed back to her desk, shut down her computer and told her boss she'd be back in the morning. When she made it to the front door, Damon stood beside his idling dark blue Lexus.

He held the car door open for her. When he'd slid into the driver's seat and pulled out into the car park traffic, she asked, "Where is this gallery?"

"You'll see."

They traveled in silence; she could think of nothing

to say. She couldn't start the conversation about finalizing things until she'd seen what he had to show her. And there was nothing else to talk about.

Her gaze flicked to Damon and she noted the tense set of his shoulders, the way his hands gripped the wheel a little too firmly. She frowned. Why wasn't he trying to convince her to come back? Why wasn't he trying to touch her?

He pulled the car to a stop and swung into a roadside parking space in an up-market section of town, where several private galleries were located. She knew the rent was through the roof in this area. Glancing up and down the street a large, simple bronze shop front caught her eye. *Lily's Place—Opening Soon.*

Damon stepped from the car and walked around to open her door.

She swallowed, confused. "What…" But she didn't know how to finish the sentence. Too many questions to choose one to lead with.

"I'll let your grandmother explain."

Damon opened the gallery door with his key and they walked in through the secure entranceway. The airy, white room still had boxes with packing materials spread across the floor, but several sculptures in glass cases were displayed on podiums.

Drawn to them, she moved, barely aware her feet were in motion. She ran a finger along one glass case, her art-curator's eye appreciating the simple beauty of the carved marble figures.

She turned to where Damon waited, but noticed the painting on the wall beside him was a portrait of a Victorian woman, surrounded by children dressed as small adults. The one that had hung in Travis Blakely's private gallery.

"That painting is yours." She forced words through a tight throat, willing reality to return.

"It was mine. I signed it, and all the other contents of my uncle's gallery, over to your gran a few days ago. They belong here, where people can see them. Not trapped in a dark room."

Damon surveyed the painting wistfully. "Hidden," he murmured, as if to himself. "Unappreciated."

As he'd been? Confused again, her mind warning her not to believe, yet her heart aching to, she looked him over. Yes, there was something different about him. He'd given her a gift she actually wanted.

The old Damon wouldn't have even known what she wanted, nor would he have cared to find out. In his world, what he decided was best for her was always the right thing.

But now, it was as if he'd come out into the light as well, ended the years of being trapped, first by an unscrupulous uncle, and then by his own plans of revenge.

Becoming the man he would have been, had his parents lived…

A door opened from the back of the gallery and Gran shuffled in. She looked radiant—more alive than Lily had seen her in years.

"Darling," she called to Lily.

Lily rushed over and embraced her in a tight hug. "Gran, why didn't you tell me you were doing this?"

Gran looked over her shoulder at Damon. "Your

husband asked me to keep it a secret. He wanted to surprise you."

Slowly Lily turned to look at Damon, then back to Gran. Wanting, wishing—not daring to believe. "So what, exactly, has he done?"

"He set up the business side and donated his uncle's collection. He also gave us a fund for purchasing new artwork."

"A fund?" Lily's mind immediately sprang to conditions on the money Damon would have set—a lever for future manipulations. "What are the strings?"

She felt Damon move up behind her. "No strings. I sold BlakeCorp and put the money into a fund for Lily's Place. Your gran is the only signatory at the moment."

She must have heard him wrong. *He'd sold Blake-Corp?* It'd been his life's ambition. "You sold it?"

"I'd already won—taking it back from the old vulture. But it was a hollow victory." He looked into her eyes with that unashamed pain and yearning and regret, and she knew his meaning. She knew because it was the same for her. Her success at being independent was empty without sharing it with the one she loved.

Her hands fluttered up. "But selling it is so extreme…"

"I didn't want the reminder. BlakeCorp is my past. The last thing I need is a constant symbol of my mistakes. Far better it be of some use here."

Now the fervent promptings of her heart grew louder than the warnings of her mind. Could it be? Were this leopard's spots changing before her eyes?

He cleared his throat. "There's one more thing I want to show you. Come with me."

Mind in a whirl, she turned to Gran, who said, "Go on, darling. At least look at what he wants to show you."

Lily took a deep breath. In for a penny, in for a pound. She turned back to Damon and nodded.

He turned for the door and she followed, waving a quick goodbye to Gran with a promise to be back soon.

Damon tucked her into the car and pulled out onto the road. Again, they were quiet on the trip, Lily too bewildered to form coherent thoughts or questions, and Damon once more holding the wheel with white knuckles, the muscles of his neck corded.

As they turned into the street of the old Blakely mansion, she spoke tightly. "I've seen your house before, Damon."

"Bear with me a little longer." He turned into the circular drive and she noticed something odd. The front lawn was covered in new garden beds—all filled with spring blossoms. There were daffodils, roses and daisies, and one large bed in the middle was filled with lilies. Day lilies, peace lilies, climbing lilies and African lilies.

She caught her breath. From death to life… "How…how did you do this so quickly?"

"You just have to know who to ask." Still grim, he turned off the ignition and came around to her door. "Come in. Please."

She stepped out and took his hand, unrelenting surprise not allowing her to think clearly. Her gaze swept the front of the mansion, which she'd once thought so imposing. It now had a veranda added to the top story, softening the edges of its profile.

Damon led her to the door where Thomas waited, a look of relief spreading across his face. "You found her!"

Thomas reached forward and, for the second time since she'd met him, hugged her. "Welcome home, Mrs. Blakely. The place hasn't been the same since you left." He stepped back, face beaming with delight. "And now it will never be the same again!"

Lily opened her mouth to stop his train of thought from where it was going, but Damon had shrugged out of his coat, rolled up his sleeves and headed down the hall. She managed a quick wiggle of her fingers to the cheerful Thomas before they turned the corner and she lost sight of him and the door.

Damon opened the first door on the left, the formal dining room. But it wasn't formal anymore, it was full of life and informality and…love. And it looked eerily similar to the design she'd sketched for this room.

"How did you know?"

"I found your sketches after you left."

She walked in, touching the back of a wooden chair with a bright lemon cushion, running her fingers along the edge of the slab wood table. "Why?"

He gripped the back of a chair and gazed out the window for a moment before meeting her eyes. "When I found your sketches, I saw the house through your eyes. I saw its potential instead of its past. It was time for me to let go."

She thought she knew what he meant, but needed to hear it from him. "Let go?"

He walked to the window, leaning against the frame as he answered, speaking slowly. "Travis was a sadistic brute. But I've been giving him power by holding on to my anger. By transforming this house to your vision, I've reclaimed a part of myself." He pushed off the wall to stand straight and tall. "I won't let him own me."

Joy for him, for his liberty, spread from her heart to her toes and fingertips. "When? How?"

"It was you, Lily." His voice was rough, his gaze intense. "*You've* changed me."

Tears filled her eyes and she took a step toward him, but he forestalled her.

"Let's keep going."

He took her to room after room, each transformed according to her vision. She couldn't help it—the tears streamed silently down her cheeks now.

The last room was the nursery. "How did you get it done so soon?"

"I called in five teams of interior decorators. Thomas oversaw them and John oversaw the gardening team." He spread his hands. "There's still a lot more to do—the south wing hasn't been touched yet—but at least it's a home now, Lily. A home for you and the baby. You've created this."

She picked up a cuddly teddy and held it to her chest before replacing it in the crib. "No, you created it. I just had the ideas."

"Let's say *we* created it. It only needs you and our baby here. And me." Finally, at last, he touched her, his hands capturing hers, his eyes dark and pleading. "I love you, Lily. I *need* you. I've confronted the ghosts that had been haunting me, thanks to you. You gave me the template to transform myself as surely as you gave me one for the house."

She sniffed and blinked, wanting to brush the tears aside, but to do so would mean letting go of his hands, and she wasn't letting him go again. Ever. "Damon, I'm so proud of you," she whispered through a ball of aching joy in her throat.

"Wait, there's one more room I want to show you." Still grabbing tight hold of her hand, he set off for the rear of the house, almost at a run. She laughed as she rushed to keep up.

He pushed through the double doors of the mansion's private gallery, but inside it was empty.

"Everything has gone to Gran's gallery," she said.

Damon dug his hands deep into his pockets and met her gaze. "I always had an interest in art as a child. It started when this gallery was a place of refuge from my aunt and uncle. I read books about art, learned on my own."

"So that's why you knew about Monet's cathedrals."

"Yes."

"But what happened? Why didn't you follow up on your interest?"

He cleared his throat. "Travis found me here hiding one day." His hand absentmindedly ran over a scar on his left arm.

Oh, God. Her heart bled as if pierced with a dagger. She'd thought it was a *sporting* injury. She gently brushed the scar with her fingers, as if to soothe the damage. "He did that to you?"

She'd known life must have been horrible for Damon as a young boy but she'd never truly faced how grim things were until seeing and understanding the full force of this evidence now.

Damon looked at the mark, seemingly surprised at the information he'd given away. "Yes." He shrugged.

She leaned down and gently kissed his scarred forearm, then wrapped both hands around it. "I'm glad he's gone, or I'd kill him myself."

He searched her eyes, then a ghost of a smile flitted across his face. "Afterward—" his voice was hoarse as he threaded his fingers through hers "—even this room was tainted. I gave up my interest in art, but you allowed me to reclaim that, as well."

All thoughts of Travis instantly gone, joy bubbled up and overflowed. Damon may have given her gifts today, but more, he'd shown that *she'd* given *him* something priceless. No longer did she feel useless, a decoration in his life…or unloved. "Damon."

He swallowed. "You know your gran has dreams of employing you to run the gallery. Be the curator. You could select staff, take the baby to work with you. Choose your own hours. Or help her find a curator if you'd rather stay at home and be a full-time mother." He shrugged. "I could even help look after the baby. I'd like that—if you want."

The options opening before her were wonderful. Miraculous. And she melted just a little more inside at his hopes of helping with their baby. "I can't think of a single person who'd be better with our baby. But one more thing. Tell me you didn't really sell BlakeCorp. It meant more to you than anything."

He turned to her, his eyes fierce. "*You* mean more to me than anything. You and our child. I didn't want any question of that. I still have my own company and I'll still probably work long hours, but I swear to you, Lily, I'll always put you first. You'll be my number one priority…if you'll have me."

She bit her lip and took a small step closer to his heat and essence and solidity. "You truly sold Blake-Corp…for me?"

He leaned in that last inch and encircled her in his arms. "I'd do anything for you. Anything." His voice rasped with raw emotion. "Tell me I got this right, Lily. Tell me I've given you what you want most. If I didn't, just ask me for it and I'll give it to you."

"You just did. All I ever wanted was you, all of you." She hugged him tight, overcome by the emotion. "I love you, Damon. More than I thought I could bear. I've been in my own private hell loving you so much but not being able to be with you. You're all I want—you, me and our baby. Our family."

He pulled back, and his whole face broke out in the kind of smile she'd never seen from him before—just simple happiness, no shadows of the past haunting him at last. "There's nothing I want more than that, either. To live with you and our child in our home. Except…"

Her heart skipped a full beat. "Except?"

"Except maybe to live in our home with you, our baby and our next baby."

She grinned, and threw herself into his arms, holding him tight. "Oh, yes, that's a vision of the future I can support."

He lifted her chin for his kiss and she sighed, not needing a single thing more than what was in the room with her at that moment.

Epilogue

Lily finished wrapping the oil painting she'd just sold and looked up to check on Pearl. In her favorite pink "gall'ry" dress—floor length, with a full "twirling skirt"—her three-year-old daughter was dancing across the room, showing an elderly couple around Lily's Place.

A laugh of pure love escaped. She could barely believe her life, and her child's, was so perfect. Five years ago, she never would have dared to dream so big.

"She's sweet. Is she yours?" The businessman in front of the counter smiled and took the wrapped package.

"Yes, she is." Lily beamed at her customer as she returned his credit card with his receipt. "Enjoy your painting."

Maree, the full-time saleswoman, was talking to a middle-aged woman, and four other people browsed quietly through the permanent display section in the next room, so Lily sneaked over to eavesdrop on her youngest saleswoman in action.

The elderly man was looking at the landscape Pearl pointed to, and the woman leaned down to ask Pearl, "Why do you like it so much?"

Without missing a beat, her eyes wide with the importance of the conversation, Pearl replied, "It's got nice purple at a-top."

Both customers lifted their gazes to the top of the painting. The man nodded. "She's right. That pale lavender in the distance balances the painting's depth and palette perfectly."

Lily's heart swelled with pride. She supposed it was hardly surprising Pearl picked up knowledge about art after the amount of time she'd spent in the gallery since her birth, but she seemed to have an incredible affinity with colors and composition for a three-year-old.

A whoosh to her left caught Lily's attention as the front door slid open and Damon strode in, gorgeous in a charcoal business suit, pushing a baby buggy. Lily's breath caught in her throat at the sight of him and their baby. A love for her husband swelled up, so big it felt as if it overflowed her heart, spilling into the air around her.

"Daddee!" Pearl ran across the tiled floor and launched herself at Damon, who caught her in an effortless move and swung her into the air.

Lily's face broke into a smile. She loved her work in

the gallery two afternoons a week, but her favorite time of the day was when Damon dropped in with baby Michael to pick them up, and she had her husband and two beautiful children in one place. Damon had been so supportive—delegating work and taking one afternoon off to allow Lily this time in the gallery. The other afternoon, today, Gran had Michael, and Damon collected him on the way home.

Damon sidestepped the buggy, still with Pearl in one arm, and reached for Lily. "Sweetheart," he murmured before kissing her lips slowly and tenderly.

Lily melted as the familiar rush of desire almost made her knees buckle. His effect on her had only deepened over the years—she could still barely stand to see him and not touch him, even if just holding his hand. She wound an arm around his neck and held him closer.

"I missed you," he said against her lips.

"And me?" Pearl chirped. "Did you miss me?"

Damon's smile for their daughter made Lily's heart sing. "And you, munchkin. So much that Michael and I had to come and get you."

"Yay!" Pearl hugged her dad tighter as Damon released Lily to push the buggy through the gallery and into the staff area out the back.

He checked on Michael, who was sleeping soundly, then deposited Pearl back on the ground. "And to give you some news."

Lily glanced at her darling eight-month-old, her fingers twitching to pick him up, but hating to disturb his sleep.

"News?" Pearl asked, voice excited.

Damon nodded. "Gran is coming over to spend the night with you and Michael."

Lily smiled and her skin tingled with anticipation. Another of Damon's impromptu nights out. She could never guess when the next one was coming or where they'd be.

"In fact, Gran is at our house now." He turned from Pearl to Lily, and dropped his voice. "So we just need to change and then we're going out."

Gran's health had improved so much, probably from a lack of stress as much as anything. But still, it was reassuring to know that Thomas and Melissa—who now worked together in running the household—would be around to do any work, leaving Gran to have fun with Pearl and Michael.

"So what should I wear? Where are we going?"

He grinned, used to her fishing for their destination. "Dress up...but make sure it comes off easily." His gaze turned to smoldering as he raked it up and down her body.

Lily glanced over at Pearl, who was busy packing up her lunchbox and toys. Then she took a step forward and ran a finger down her husband's chest, pleased by his sharp intake of breath at her provocative move.

She blinked innocently. "There's nothing I can do to convince you to give me a hint?"

He captured her finger and pulled it up to his mouth, biting gently on the tip, and she felt the touch down to her core. "Choose shoes you can wear in the helicopter," he rasped. "And, sweetheart, be prepared to follow through on that promise in your eyes."

She laughed, low and husky. "I love being married to you, my husband."

His eyes suddenly became serious, filled with love and certainty. "And I love being married to you, my wife."

* * * * *

Don't miss Rachel's next book,
THE BLACKMAILED BRIDE'S SECRET CHILD,
available next month from Silhouette Desire.

*Fan favorite Leslie Kelly is bringing her readers
a fantasy so scandalous, we're calling it
FORBIDDEN!*

*Look for
PLAY WITH ME
Available February 2010
from Harlequin® Blaze™.*

"AREN'T YOU GOING TO SAY 'Fly me' or at least 'Welcome aboard'?"

Amanda Bauer didn't. The softly muttered word that actually came out of her mouth was a lot less welcoming. And had fewer letters. Four, to be exact.

The man shook his head and tsked. "Not exactly the friendly skies. Haven't caught the spirit yet this morning?"

"Make one more airline-slogan crack and you'll be walking to Chicago," she said.

He nodded once, then pushed his sunglasses onto the top of his tousled hair. The move revealed blue eyes that matched the sky above. And yeah. They were twinkling. Damn it.

"Understood. Just, uh, promise me you'll say 'Coffee, tea or me' at least once, okay? Please?"

Amanda tried to glare, but that twinkle sucked the annoyance right out of her. She could only draw in a slow breath as he climbed into the plane. As she watched her passenger disappear into the small jet, she had to wonder about the trip she was about to take.

Coffee and tea they had, and he was welcome to them. But her? Well, she'd never even considered making a move on a customer before. Talk about unprofessional.

And yet…

Something inside her suddenly wanted to take a chance, to be a little outrageous.

How long since she had done indecent things—or decent ones, for that matter—with a sexy man? Not since before they'd thrown all their energies into expanding Clear-Blue Air, at the very least. She hadn't had time for a lunch date, much less the kind of lust-fest she'd enjoyed in her younger years. The kind that lasted for entire weekends and involved not leaving a bed except to grab the kind of sensuous food that could be smeared onto—and eaten off—someone else's hot, naked, sweat-tinged body.

She closed her eyes, her hand clenching tight on the railing. Her heart fluttered in her chest and she tried to make herself move. But she couldn't—not climbing up, but not backing away, either. Not physically, and not in her head.

Was she really considering this? God, she hadn't even looked at the stranger's left hand to make sure he was available. She had no idea if he was actually attracted to her or just an irrepressible flirt. Yet something inside was telling her to take a shot with this man.

It was crazy. Something she'd never considered. Yet right now, at this moment, she was definitely considering it. If he was available…could she do it? Seduce a stranger. Have an anonymous fling, like something out of a blue movie on late-night cable?

She didn't know. All she knew was that the flight to Chicago was a short one so she had to decide quickly. And as she put her foot on the bottom step and began to climb up, Amanda suddenly had to wonder if she was about to embark on the ride of her life.

HARLEQUIN® *Blaze*™

*It all started
with a few naughty books....*

As a member of the Red Tote Book Club,
Carol Snow has been studying works of
classic erotic literature…but Carol doesn't
believe in love…or marriage. It's going to take
another kind of classic—Charles Dickens's
A Christmas Carol—and a little otherworldly
persuasion to convince her to go after her
own sexily ever after.

Cuddle up with

Her Sexy Valentine

by STEPHANIE BOND

Available February 2010

---

red-hot reads

HARLEQUIN
Ambassadors

Want to share your passion for reading Harlequin® Books?

Become a Harlequin Ambassador!

Harlequin Ambassadors are a group of passionate and well-connected readers who are willing to share their joy of reading Harlequin® books with family and friends.

You'll be sent all the tools you need to spark great conversation, including free books!

All we ask is that you share the romance with your friends and family!

You'll also be invited to have a say in new book ideas and exchange opinions with women just like you!

To see if you qualify* to be a Harlequin Ambassador, please visit www.HarlequinAmbassadors.com.

*Please note that not everyone who applies to be a Harlequin Ambassador will qualify. For more information please visit www.HarlequinAmbassadors.com.

Thank you for your participation.

BAP09BPA

REQUEST YOUR FREE BOOKS!

2 FREE NOVELS
PLUS 2
FREE GIFTS!

Silhouette

Desire ®

Passionate, Powerful, Provocative!

YES! Please send me 2 FREE Silhouette Desire® novels and my 2 FREE gifts (gifts are worth about $10). After receiving them, if I don't wish to receive any more books, I can return the shipping statement marked "cancel." If I don't cancel, I will receive 6 brand-new novels every month and be billed just $4.05 per book in the U.S. or $4.74 per book in Canada. That's a saving of almost 15% off the cover price! It's quite a bargain! Shipping and handling is just 50¢ per book in the U.S. and 75¢ per book in Canada.* I understand that accepting the 2 free books and gifts places me under no obligation to buy anything. I can always return a shipment and cancel at any time. Even if I never buy another book, the two free books and gifts are mine to keep forever.

225 SDN E39X 326 SDN E4AA

Name	(PLEASE PRINT)

Address	Apt. #

City	State/Prov.	Zip/Postal Code

Signature (if under 18, a parent or guardian must sign)

Mail to the **Silhouette Reader Service:**

IN U.S.A.: P.O. Box 1867, Buffalo, NY 14240-1867
IN CANADA: P.O. Box 609, Fort Erie, Ontario L2A 5X3

Not valid for current subscribers to Silhouette Desire books.

Want to try two free books from another line?
Call 1-800-873-8635 or visit www.morefreebooks.com.

* Terms and prices subject to change without notice. Prices do not include applicable taxes. N.Y. residents add applicable sales tax. Canadian residents will be charged applicable provincial taxes and GST. Offer not valid in Quebec. This offer is limited to one order per household. All orders subject to approval. Credit or debit balances in a customer's account(s) may be offset by any other outstanding balance owed by or to the customer. Please allow 4 to 6 weeks for delivery. Offer available while quantities last.

Your Privacy: Silhouette Books is committed to protecting your privacy. Our Privacy Policy is available online at www.eHarlequin.com or upon request from the Reader Service. From time to time we make our lists of customers available to reputable third parties who may have a product or service of interest to you. If you would prefer we not share your name and address, please check here. ☐

Help us get it right—We strive for accurate, respectful and relevant communications. To clarify or modify your communication preferences, visit us at www.ReaderService.com/consumerchoice.

SDES10